Called into Question

Paul Canon Harris

Introduction

"Called into Question" is a work of fiction and all the characters in the story are products of my imagination. Any resemblance to persons living or dead is accidental. As with any story or other creative work imagination and experience combine.

In publishing this book, I salute the many fine women and men I know who have served or still serve as police officers. The few so-called "bad apples" undermine their good work and sadly, have a disproportionate effect on the reputation of the police.

I also want to thank the team of friends who have encouraged me in my writing and who have critiqued the fruits of my labour at different stages.

Paul Canon Harris
Bournemouth
April 2018

Chapter 1

Bruce glanced at his watch anxiously. He was uncertain whether this meeting was a good idea or not. If the other two showed up it would be the first time they had been together for nearly three years. Memories of that momentous summer were still strong and haunting. Bruce was certain that his former colleague would come but what about her? She was another story, very much her own woman in her own world, knowing her mind and with her own agenda. He had chosen this corner table carefully. Sitting with his back to the wall, he felt secure. He could not be taken by surprise. He had a clear view of both entrances.

At five past eleven a smart young Asian man came in. Bruce stood up smiling and extended his hand towards his friend who took it and returned a firm handshake. The two men looked each other in the eye; the mutual respect and trust were still there. "Harpal. So good to see you. Not like you to be late. Standards slipping?"

"Ha! Very funny! Glad to see you're on form. Traffic was terrible."

"Have a seat." Bruce said. "Shall we order, or should we hang on until she gets here?"

"Don't you mean *if* she gets here? I'm still not sure she'll come. I thought she'd decided to make a clean break with our Cheston days."

"That's what I thought too, but she replied to my card and said she would try and make it. But, you're right, ever the gentleman, it'll look rude if we've started." Bruce sat down at the table, still watching the door.

Ten minutes later she arrived, striking in a casual outfit, tight blue jeans, brown suede Chelsea boots and a navy sailing smock. A blue and pink scarf knotted
extravagantly in her hair completed the arty look. She smiled sheepishly at the men. That coy smile took Bruce back immediately to the first time he had seen her. Water had flowed under many bridges since that first night.

Bruce ordered drinks and they sat quiet for a moment, each of them stunned by the powerful mix of emotions this meeting triggered. The exchange of a few pleasantries jump-started the conversation. "You're both looking well. How often do you get to see each other?" asked the girl.

"Not very often – I am only back in the area two or three times a year and he's always busy with their business. So, this is a rare occasion, the more so because of you being here. To be honest, Harpal and I wondered whether you might stand us up."

"At least you could have consoled each other," she replied, "Shall we order?"

"Still quick on your feet when you need to be, I see." laughed Bruce.

"And you haven't lost your way with words."

Called into Question

Bruce blushed and signaled to the waitress.

"Talking of special occasions," said Harpal, "I have an announcement to make. I am going to become a father."

"Wow, that's brilliant. Congratulations." Bruce clapped him on the shoulder.

"That's lovely news," said the girl. "when's the baby due?"

"Early April," replied Harpal glowing with pride.

"A spring baby. Exciting times ahead then. Well done the pair of you. And what about you Bruce – how are things with you now?" The girl's concerned expression was at odds with the casual tone of her voice.

"I'm better than I was thanks. My shoulder only hurts occasionally but the medics tell me that's normal with scar tissue. Most of the time I am fine."

"What about the flashbacks? Are they still troubling you?" Harpal asked, recalling his own vivid memories of the incident.

"Not really, not as bad as they were."

The mental flashbacks had troubled Bruce more than his physical wounds. Flashbacks – they were well-named! Sometimes it seemed like only yesterday he had joined the force.

Chapter 2

Bruce Hammond looked at the enormous wooden doors. There was no bell to be seen. With butterflies in his stomach and a strong sense of taking his future in his hands he grasped the large, black, lion-shaped door knocker. He rapped twice. It was louder than he had intended and made him jump. "Go around the side you pregnant elf!" barked someone sharply from the other side. Bruce looked back to the gravel car park where he had parked his white Mini and saw a sign by a gap in the yew hedge. "All recruits this way." It was not an auspicious start to his police career.

Eynsham Hall, a Jacobean-style stately home surrounded by acres of lush Oxfordshire parkland was to be his home for the next three months. The impressive building had been a base for Barclays Bank, then the RAF, and finally had served as a maternity hospital before becoming a training centre where police recruits cut their teeth.

Bruce had spent the previous week with twelve other new recruits at the Thames Valley Police training centre in a similar but slightly smaller country pile near Reading. They had been issued with uniform and personal equipment. The ten men had all been shorn of their hair. They resembled Dickensian convicts. The three women had got off lightly. A rather plain woman instructor had showed them how to pile and pin their locks in such a way as to minimize sexuality and maximize severity. The week had included one whole morning exploring the benefits of the Police Mutual Pensions scheme. Some of the older recruits had been impressed and nodded sagely.

Called into Question

For Bruce, who had just turned nineteen, talk of retirement dates and annuities was like hearing a language from a country he never expected to visit. At the end of the week they had been sworn in by a solemn local magistrate, thereby officially becoming police officers with uniforms, numbers and little clue as to what they could and could not do.

On the Friday they learned where they would be posted after they had completed their basic training. Bruce was pleasantly surprised to learn that he would be based in Cheston, near his home. He felt relieved, knowing that he could have been posted to somewhere like Bletchley in the north or way beyond Reading in the west. One of the women recruits was tearful; she had been hoping to be deployed in the south of the area where her boy-friend was a Detective Constable. The powers-that-be had decided distance was a necessity in their case. With their futures opening before them for better or worse they had been sent home for weekend leave. They were to report on the following Monday to various Home Office Training Centres where they would spend the twelve weeks up to Christmas with recruits from other forces being knocked into the required shape.

Bruce had driven up that morning through the Chilterns from his family home near Cheston. It was bright and fresh, beech trees turning copper and gold to welcome the new season. The Oxfordshire countryside had glistened, opening out before him as he came through the motorway cut at Stokenchurch. The weekend had felt surreal, an uncomfortable lull before the storm. His fiancée Jenny, a student nurse, had been working most of the weekend. She had come over on Sunday afternoon, but their time together had been strained and full of interruptions from his two younger sisters, Hannah and Sarah, who were desperate to play with his truncheon and handcuffs. Hannah, the younger of the two becoming stuck in the cuffs for over an hour had done little to lighten the mood.

'Name, force and number?' The sergeant did not look up from his clipboard and list.

'Bruce Hammond, Thames Valley, PC1066'

'1066 what?'

'Sorry, I don't understand.' Bruce could feel himself blushing.

'You will be sorry with a number like that.1066… *Sergeant!* Have you got that Hastings?'

'It's Hammond not Hastings, Sergeant.'

'I know that Hammond! Didn't they teach you any history at that poncey grammar school of yours? With that number you're going to be Hastings when you reach your nick. And take it from me you're getting off lightly. Got it?'

'Yes Sergeant.'

'You're on the top floor, Dorm 5. Take a course list and a set of sheets from over there. Make sure you are in the assembly hall at 2pm. Now push off.'

'Thank you, Sergeant.' Bruce took a pair of rough sheets and a worn pillow case from a trestle table, tucked them under his arm and struggled up three flights of what had been the backstairs for maids and butlers.

Bruce had to stoop as he reached the top floor and emerged on to a long landing with a worn blue carpet bordered by brown marbled lino. He was tall, rangy and athletic. The dark stubble on his head showed his hair was normally thick and black. He had inherited his Latin looks from his mother Sophia. She was Italian and had come to England in 1947 when her ex-POW father had decided to make a new life for his family in the land of his captivity. He had been held at Kempton Park racecourse, and after digging vegetables on Clapham Common and building prefabricated houses in Catford he had chosen the fog and rain of south London over the warmth, the colours and the corruption of Calabria!

Sophia would have returned to Italy had she not fallen in love with a young art student. Muir Hammond, was himself an exile in London, living a long way away from the family farm in the Scottish borders. Thrown together at ballroom dancing lessons they had enjoyed a whirlwind romance, married in spring 1954 and celebrated Bruce's birth the following year. Landscape painting remained a life-long passion for his father, but it did not pay the bills. In 1960 Bruce's father had applied, and after two years of training, had been accepted for ministry in the Methodist church.

So, Bruce had become a son of the Manse, something which did not sit easily with him as he exchanged the certainties of childhood for the realities of adult life. Methodists moved their ministers on like clockwork every five years, in theory to avoid stagnation or over-attachment. His father used to joke, "After five years, if the person's any good, it's time someone else had them; and if they aren't any good, it's time someone else had them!" Either way, Bruce had been unimpressed when in 1971 the family left the excitement of the city and moved into a respectable but sleepy Berkshire village in sight of Windsor castle and in the flight path of Heathrow.

Despite his initial reluctance, Bruce had settled into his new environment and flourished at the local grammar school, shining academically and on the sports field. His teachers and parents had assumed he would go to university and possibly even try for Oxford or Cambridge. His announcement that he had applied to go into the police straight after his A-levels did not go down well. His father was of the view that he would be a thoroughbred among cart horses. In an awkward interview his headmaster told him in no uncertain terms that he was wasting his ability. Neither had been impressed by Bruce's argument that by going in at nineteen he could be on the Accelerated Promotion course within two years, thereby gaining an advantage over those who chose the graduate entry scheme. He was not slow in expressing his self-confidence. However, he found it harder to admit, even to himself, that the thought of setting up home with Jenny in a police house was a major factor in the decision-making process.

Bruce stepped into the large dormitory. With its eaves and gabled-windows it was not an ideal room for a group of men who were all, by definition, above average height. There were six metal framed beds, each one flanked by a utility style bedside cabinet on one side and a wardrobe on the other. The rough standard issue blankets and items of uniform around the room gave Bruce the surreal sensation of having stepped back into a war-time barracks room.

"Wotcha, you can choose from one of those two. The others are all taken mate. I'm Pete Harmston, City of London."

Bruce shook the offered hand. "Bruce Hammond, Thames Valley." He put his sheets and case on the bed in the corner furthest from the door. He hung his uniform in its cover on the outside of his wardrobe, sat down on the bed and surveyed the room. Of the other three room-mates, two were from Essex Police and one from the Bedfordshire force. They appeared a few years older than him and seemed quite at ease in their new settings. Bruce suspected that they may have been ex-servicemen.

"Matey boy from Norfolk is last to come," said Pete Harmston reading from the room list. "His tractor's probably broken down. You're a jammy git training in your own area ain't you? You got bawled out for using the wrong door. We saw you coming down the drive. You've got the white 1275GT."

Bruce nodded. Harmston was clearly going to be an observant police officer.

"How long did it take you in that? They can really shift." asked Bedfordshire.

"Only about an hour from near Cheston. That new M40 makes it a doddle." In fact, Bruce had driven more slowly than normal, acutely aware of how ironic it would be to be pulled over for speeding on this of all days.

At this point a cheery-looking face appeared round the door frame. "Dorm 5?" It was immediately apparent from the broad accent that this was the missing tractor driver from Norfolk. He came in and flopped on the bed. "What a pissin' nightmare of a journey that was!" Bruce and the others had to suppress a laugh at the accent which was, at one and the same time, engaging and comic.
"Go on you boys, laugh, I don't mind. Used to it."

Just before two o'clock the old building echoed to the sound of fifty pairs of feet making their way down the wooden staircases. They filed into the assembly hall, a room of gracious proportions, with views over the formal gardens to the parkland beyond. Bruce imagined that the recesses in the panelled walls might once have housed Landseer or Constable paintings. Now, fading aerial views of various police headquarters alternated round the room with garish wooden shields of force badges. His sense of the incongruous was heightened by the grey tubular metal and canvas stacking chairs on which the recruits sat.

The Commandant, a florid Chief Superintendent whose straining uniform suggested that the sedentary nature of his role was gaining the upper hand in the battle with his waist line, sat on a wooden platform at the end of the room. His team of instructors flanked him on either side, sitting four to a trestle table surveying their latest batch of victims. They were sergeants seconded from different forces. One of them sported a red sash, the significance of which was revealed as one by one they introduced themselves. Bruce reflected that the scene was faintly reminiscent of University Challenge. "Sergeant Higgins, Essex Police, reading sexual offences!"

Red Sash turned out to be the Drill Sergeant who was on a one-man mission to make all recruits wonder how they had managed to live so long without the joys of square-bashing, boot-bulling, and steam-pressing. Bruce tried unsuccessfully to banish a mental image of attempted arrests on the local streets being ruined by him and his colleagues approaching at double quick time three abreast accompanied by cries of "left, right, left, right". The more he thought about it the more like something out of Monty Python it became.

"For the next twelve weeks, this is your home, and this should be your focus. Don't see this as something simply to be endured, a hoop to jump through. Your police career begins here. My aim is that when you pass out of here you will look like police officers, think like police officers, and will act as police officers. We shall be watching you like hawks. My report will go to your home forces." The Commandant was in full flow. "During the week your feet will barely touch the ground. When you go home at weekends do not think for one moment that your time is your own. You can warn your wives and girlfriends not to expect too much weekend fun or hanky panky. You will be revising hard for your Monday exam on the previous week's topic." Bruce sensed he was building up to a big theatrical finish. "Finally let me remind you, gentlemen, that I have the power to dismiss you from the course, and therefore from the Police Service if you fall short in any way of the required standards." His parting shot delivered, he stood up and exited stage left, leaving the instructors to spell out in detail the shape of a week.

The training would include law, physical fitness, running, self-defence, swimming, life-saving, first aid and drill. The Physical Training Instructor, a heavily built man with a lazy eye that made him look like comedian Marty Feldman's muscular big brother was clearly intent on being every bit as intimidating as the Drill Sergeant. "Some of you may think you are fit now, but by the time you finish here you will be as hard and lean as a butcher's dog. If you are a non-swimmer now you will learn to swim. You will all leave here with a life-saving qualification. You will run the Stamina Run against the clock three times a week and I do not, repeat do not, accept sick notes! The self-defence we do here is Aikido and you ex-squaddies can forget about pulling a fast one on me."

Bruce relished the prospect of so much sport. He was keen to be selected for the Force football team. He also hoped to burn off some of his pent-up frustration, the result of having had so little time alone with Jenny recently.

The Drill Sergeant brought the session to a close and Bruce stood up to file out. He was taken aback to hear his name barked out. "PC's Hammond, Harmston, Trendell and Wilkins come and see me here now." Wondering immediately what he had done wrong he made his way to the front of the room. The four of them stood trying to look relaxed yet conscious of the gazes of their departing colleagues. "Don't look so frightened!" said the

Called into Question

sergeant. "Each of you has been selected to act as a class leader. And before your heads swell let me assure you, you may regret this. If your class foul up on the parade ground or in the practical sessions, you will be held responsible. That means we deduct marks from your personal assessment. Do you understand?" They nodded without meeting his eye as he handed each of them a blue shoulder lanyard. "Your cards have clearly been marked, God only knows why from the look of you. Now go and introduce yourselves to your class mates. Good luck – you'll need it!"

Chapter 3

Training institutions, whether military or civilian, have a culture that is peculiarly their own. This is by design and serves the purpose of moulding the recruits or trainees into the likeness of the parent organization. Eynsham Hall was no exception. The golden days of autumn passed at a highly regimented pace. At the heart of the programme was a weekly topic covering different aspects of law and police process. Bruce assimilated information readily and the weekly multiple-choice tests on a Monday morning were a very light intellectual work-out compared with his A-levels. For many of his class-mates however, preparing for these examinations blighted their weekend leave. Conversation over Monday lunch was dominated by discussing the questions and comparing answers. Hindsight and the consensus left most recruits at some point with the sick-feeling that the recognition of a mistake or an omission brings.

The sense of being back at primary school that Bruce had experienced on his first day was reinforced by the inter-class competition. The instructors awarded and deducted points at any opportunity. If the Drill Sergeant decided that a class squad was late on the Parade Square in the morning, points were lost. The daily uniform inspection gave plenty of opportunity for him and the Commandant to indulge their petty delight in picking up on the tiniest detail – a speck of fluff on a tunic or a mark on a polished toe-cap. Bruce had quickly realized that assembling his class in advance and getting one of the ex-squaddies to do a pre-inspection saved points and no little grief on the parade square. Every activity from class-room tests, through to football matches and first aid lectures carried a points potential. During one of the Friday afternoon gatherings, at which the points tally for the week were updated on a large pegboard, Bruce wondered whether such a pre-occupation with keeping scores was a sign of an anally-retentive, emotionally retarded organization? He recalled that back in the day at Primary School Romans – the yellow house always seemed to have the edge over the Vikings, Trojans and Spartans. He had been ten years old then.

The inter-class points league was in addition to the detailed marking of individual recruits. This was altogether more serious. The Commandant operated a "three strikes and you're out" approach to recruits' performance in the weekly tests. Failing a weekly assessment or a practical exam put pressure on a recruit. Other aspects of the regime were even more draconian. Loss of temper could lead to immediate dismissal and the team of instructors knew exactly which pressure points to press.

On Wednesday mornings Bruce's class went straight from morning parade into a practical session. There was no opportunity to change out of their best drill uniforms and into their second sets. Bruce had identified this early on as being one of the most vulnerable points of the week. The practical sessions took place in or around the frontages of four buildings which looked as though they had been lifted straight from Pinewood Studios or the set of Coronation Street. The terrace comprised two small family homes, a shop and pub. This combination provided more than enough scope for the instructors to act out scenarios to test the knowledge, initiative and character of the men in their charge. Two or three of the class would have to deal with whatever was presented to them while their classmates looked on. Instructors, some of whom appeared to be frustrated actors, hammed up their parts and went out of their way to intimidate the recruits. Smiling or giggling while dealing with the incident incurred a points deduction, losing one's cool meant dismissal. Instructors when asked for their character's name would give fictitious ones such as Ivor Bigun or John Thomas. Keeping a straight face was particularly difficult when dealing with a burly instructor in drag asking if "she" could see the size of your truncheon! In some scenarios, they would try and provoke a reaction or would resist an arrest.

In only the second week of the course Bruce's class lost their first member. The PE instructor was playing the part of a drunk who had been thrown out of the pub and had been provoking passers-by and urinating on the street. The PC dealing with the incident was Jeff who had served in the Army for five years including a tour of duty in Northern Ireland. Bruce had noted that he was naturally tough but with something of a temper on him. With the class looking on, the "drunk" became increasingly aggressive, taunting the arresting officer about his military background. It was clear that he was spoiling for a fight. As soon as Jeff went to lay a hand on him the drunk went into self-defence mode, threw him over his shoulder and into a muddy puddle to the accompaniment of gasps from the watching class. Jeff was genuinely shocked. He stood up and looked at the mud on his tunic and trousers and shouted, "You tosser, you bloody tosser – we'd have had you for breakfast in the paras!" With this he stormed off towards the main building. The class stood in stunned silence. The instructor who had been supervising the session dismissed the class. "Hammond – you will go and get your angry friend and bring him for coffee with the Dep at 11am. Understood?" Bruce nodded; "Yes Sergeant!" turned on his heel and went to find Jeff. As he walked away he could hear raised voices between the instructors.

"Coffee with the Dep" was a summary disciplinary hearing at coffee time with the Deputy Commandant. It was in reality "coffee for one!" Any course member on a charge, accompanied by their class leader, would be marched in by an instructor. The unfortunate constable, holding their helmet and white gloves under one arm would stand to attention in front of a large oak desk while details of their misdemeanour were read out. The Deputy Commandant brooked no argument and imposed a range of sanctions ranging from loss of privileges such as withdrawing welfare nights for minor infringements on the one hand, to dismissal from the course on the other. Bruce knew his classmate had sailed close the wind but was genuinely shocked when Jeff was told that his police career was over before it had started. Bruce went to speak up for his classmate. "If I want your advice PC Hammond I will ask for it. Dismiss them Sergeant please." They went back to the dormitories where Jeff started to pack his things. He now seemed remarkably calm.

"What will you do?" asked Bruce.

Jeff shrugged his shoulders. "Go on the lorries probably. HGV licence one of the best things the Army gave me. Anyways I've had enough of taking orders off pricks like them." Bruce was impressed by this calmness but reflected that this incident represented an unnecessary loss of a potentially good police officer.

Over the next few weeks there would be two further instant dismissals from the course, both thankfully from Bruce's point of view, from different classes. One officer had lost his temper in the face of extreme baiting from the PE instructor whom the recruits had nicknamed Marty. Swimming took place in the pool of a teacher training college on the edge of the city. They arrived by coach twice a week much to the amused interest of the long-haired trainee teachers in their duffel coats and bell-bottom jeans. One morning the recruits had been forced to tread water for over half-an-hour. This tested most of them but had proved too much for a spotty-faced lad from Essex who clung to the side of the pool gasping having nearly drowned. Sympathy was not on the menu, only a volley of abuse. When the unfortunate recruit had recovered sufficiently to speak he told the sergeant he could stuff his lifesaving awards where the sun didn't shine and effectively resigned on the spot.

The other casualty was someone who had drunk too much on a Welfare Night outing and had subsequently wet his bed. He endured the shame of having to carry his foam mattress across to the stores while all his colleagues were doing morning drill. He had left the premises by lunchtime.

"Welfare Night" was a euphemism for Wednesday evenings when course members were free to leave the Centre on the strict condition that they were back by 10.30pm. People usually linked up in groups of four or five and drove to nearby pubs or into Oxford ten miles away to go to a disco called Tramps in the city centre. A few, mainly older married men plus those who were gated or doing bar duty as a punishment remained, but the majority made a sharp exit, albeit a temporary one, from the hot-house.

Called into Question

With their crew cuts they looked like squaddies and were often baited by local lads looking for trouble. This weekly night out gave an opportunity to get to know two different groups of people. By a happy coincidence welfare night coincided with a regular night out for fun-loving student nurses. Bruce's course mates were ham-strung in the dating stakes by having to leave by 10pm. A fiver slipped in the direction of the DJ secured two or three slow songs which allowed an all too brief opportunity for some smooching before the witching hour. For the footloose and fancy free, this was a chance to fix a date in advance for the end of course passing out ball. Every six weeks the ever-considerate Commandant would send a coach round the nurses' halls of residence to collect willing and hopeful nurses to be the essential female element in the only time Eynsham Hall let its collective hair down. Members of the course who were completing their training scrubbed up and were kitted out in tuxedos, cummerbunds and bow ties. The course six weeks behind them acted as waiters for the evening and privately fantasized about which of the nurses on show would be their partner next time round!

Although Bruce was happy to go along and show willing with his colleagues relaxing on these weekly sorties into town, he had no interest in chasing nurses or other local girls. As far as he was concerned he had chosen his personal nurse already. He had always had an eye for the opposite sex and had started dating early by normal standards. His mother joked that she had spent two or three years consoling the girls in the church choir that her son had recently dumped. He was tall and had matured early, consequently some of his girl friends had been older than him. Contrary to his parents' suspicions and his own school-boy boasts these relationships had been innocent. Weekend parties and summer walks along the Thames had given plenty of opportunity for passionate kissing and exciting, exploratory fondling but never more than that. Something from his up-bringing had held him back. At heart Bruce was a romantic and he knew it. Then in the summer between taking his O-levels and starting A-levels, he had fallen in love with Jenny. She was two years older than him, had just left school and was spending a year working in a local nursing home before going to train as a nurse in London.

Bruce and Jenny had the next few years carefully mapped out. He could not imagine being with anyone else. She was intelligent, funny, sporty and passionate. Despite the misgivings of their parents and some friends they had got engaged as soon as Bruce left school. The plan was that they would both throw themselves in to the launch of their chosen careers and apply for a police house together after two years. They were confident that being apart would not present a problem; London was only thirty miles away and Bruce would drive up or Jenny would come home by train as often as possible. So, Welfare Nights came and went, and Bruce was a disinterested spectator as his colleagues helped Oxford's student nurses with revision for their anatomy exams.

Welfare Nights were also an opportunity for Bruce and his colleagues to get to know recruits on the course six weeks ahead of them. The pressure of the timetable at Eynsham Hall meant there was very little chance of the two courses interacting during the week. They would glimpse each other taking various classes, enduring drill instruction or tackling practicals but they were effectively segregated. There were a small number who had been cadets together in the same force and who therefore knew each other. One recruit on the course ahead stood out and Bruce had been interested to find out more about him.

Harpal Shaik was a distinguished police officer even before he had completed his basic training. He was the first person from an ethnic minority community to be recruited by Thames Valley Police. This was not a fact he shouted about, indeed the softly-spoken Shaik rarely shouted about anything. He was twenty-two and had lived in Cheston since his family had fled to England in 1968 from Kenya.

One Wednesday evening Bruce noticed Shaik sitting alone at a table overlooking the dance floor at Tramps. He was surveying the melee of girls and short-haired men gyrating beneath a giant glitter-ball to the sound of Barry White, the Bee Gees and Wings much like a professional punter watches horses in the parade ring at a race meeting. Bruce decided he would go across and introduce himself.

"Not dancing?" remarked Bruce.

"No! And I hope you're not asking." Shaik replied with a smile.

"Bruce Hammond!" Bruce offered his hand and was surprised at the strength of the other man's grip. Despite his quiet manner and soft, almost girlish good looks, there was clearly an inner strength to this man, thought Bruce as he sat down.

Harpal Shaik's family had lost the major part of their wealth which had been tied up in property in Nairobi. Harpal's older brothers and father had set about building a new commercial empire and owned two shops in Cheston but he had decided to pursue a different path.

"So how are you finding it so far? Surviving?" Shaik inquired, sipping his Canada Dry.
"So far, so good thanks. I mean some of the stuff they put on us seems petty but it's what I expected."

"I hear you're supposed to be a bit of sporting hot-shot. Good job you are as it will cut you some slack with those who will see you as a bit soft."

Bruce gave what he hoped looked like a modest shrug. He was proud of the sporting prowess that had smoothed his progress through school. He was also surprised and taken aback at Shaik's observation, the more so because he was on the other course. Clearly word travelled fast at Eynsham despite the apparent segregation.

"I'll try and give as good as I get if people think I'm soft. Anyway, what's it like for you, um, you know..." Bruce hesitated.

"Being coloured you mean? Don't be embarrassed. I'm not!"

Bruce felt awkward. There had been a significant number of boys from Asian backgrounds at school, two of whom he had got to know a little through

Called into Question

playing squash. On reflection, he realized that their conversations had been limited to school issues, he had not learned anything about their home life and what the experience of being from a minority group in society was like for them.

"It's pretty much as I expected. No great surprises. Couple of nicknames – both pretty mild compared with some stuff I've had in the past. Not really offensive – quite funny actually!"
"Like what?" Bruce was impressed with Harpal's relaxed manner. He seemed at ease with himself and in control of his emotions.

"Milk – as in milkshake and Harpic for obvious reasons. I can live with those!"

Bruce laughed. "First day the sergeant reckoned I'd be called Hastings because of my number but actually no-one's picked up on it. At school I was called Rev or Vic because my father is a minister, didn't like it at first but after a while I realized nick-names were the norm. We never used first names. If you did, you were accused of being gay! Different in 6th form, think we were a bit more secure by then."

"That's the thing to remember when you get grief off people – and you and I will get plenty of that, my friend! It is not that people are really against you. It's just the way life is. We are all insecure around people who are different." Harpal shared his insight without intensity, keeping an eye on a slim blonde in a pale blue mini-dress who was dancing near them as he spoke.

Called into Question

"Why do you think we will get grief?" asked Bruce.

"Eh, sorry, she's hot, isn't she?" Bruce followed the other man's gaze. "What did you say? Oh yeah, grief. You and are I different from most of the others on the course. I've got different skin and an accent but look at yourself you stand out from the rest as well. You're not exactly your bog-standard police recruit, are you? I know there are more guys coming in from university these days but get real, a lot of old-school coppers aren't going to like it. Even here the instructors have a go at me and it goes beyond the thing of them wanting to test us out."

Bruce nodded, realizing that he had given nothing like the thought that Harpal Shaik had given, to joining the police.

"We're both going to Cheston, we both know the area but frankly we will need to look out for each other." Harpal raised his glass. "Here's to the outsiders"
"The outsiders!" Bruce responded ruefully raising his glass of Skol.

Bruce was glad he had taken the initiative and approached Shaik. It was reassuring to know there would be another new recruit stationed in Cheston. He sensed he had made a connection and looked forward to getting to know this interesting and slightly mysterious man better.

* * * *

Called into Question

Bruce vaulted the stile and turned right along the edge of the field. Glancing over his shoulder he could see that he was thirty yards clear of the chasing pack. With breathing space, he could reflect again on his conversation with Harpal Shaik from the previous day. He had been right in his assessment. Bruce knew that his love for various sports had broken down barriers and built bridges with a wide range of people over the last few years. His athleticism and height had made him stand out. Despite his father having been a keen hockey player who in his day had represented his university, he had always encouraged Bruce in whatever sport he chose to play. He was an all-rounder but by his early teens he had settled on football and athletics as his main sports. In the winter, he was a prolific centre-forward for a local club and his school. A scout from Queens Park Rangers had taken his contact details after one game. Bruce had looked forward to a follow-up call, but it never came and he contented himself with making his mark locally. His summer passion was athletics. His physique equipped him for the demanding disciplines of the decathlon. In addition to representing his school he competed at a senior level in the Southern League for local club Cheston Harriers. He had won his county colours after coming third in the national schools' athletics championships.

His training regime involved running at least four or five times a week, usually in the early mornings. This was when he could think about his plans and his challenges in life. Having to do the stamina run three times a week was no hardship for Bruce. He had beaten the PE instructor each time with ease and had gained that resident bully's grudging respect. At school, he had read Alan Sillitoe's "The Loneliness of the Long-Distance Runner" about a boy in a borstal in the 1950's who achieved success and found inner freedom through running. Gliding over this Oxfordshire parkland that morning he smiled at the irony of a police officer and a borstal boy enjoying the same sensation of liberty through running.

After breakfast one morning in mid-October Bruce was handed an envelope by one of his class instructors who was himself from Thames Valley Police. "Open it then, Hammond! I know for a fact it's not a love letter from that girl-friend of yours." Bruce took out a flimsy sheet of blue paper. It was a carbon copy of a Squad Selection sheet for the force football team. His name was ringed in red ink. "Well done lad, pretty impressive getting picked before you've even arrived at your nick. But before it goes to your head a word to the wise! You've replaced a Detective Sergeant from Cheston CID. He's a right hard bastard, so watch yourself. The squad is picked by a couple of guys based at Reading who can't stand him. Be careful." Never had the pleasure of selection so quickly evaporated. Nevertheless, Bruce was pleased to get the news, not least because when he played he would get an additional day's pay and a day-off in lieu. One more chance for a quick trip to a London nurses' hostel!

The standard of teaching on the course was not inspiring. The sergeant instructors did their best, but Bruce could not help but compare their wooden, plodding approach to the imagination and enthusiasm of his school teachers. As the weeks went by they ticked off a range of subjects on the course menu. There was a constant theme which ran as a backdrop to the weekly topics. It was one that instructors and students had equal difficulty in grasping.

In 1967 there had been legal reforms that governed the way the police officers should conduct themselves when arresting suspects and investigating alleged crimes. The instructors, who were long-serving officers, likened these changes to the way Britain moved to decimal coinage four years later. They were not fans of either move. The changes had done away with quaintly-named crimes such as felony, had renamed them and classified them according to the power of arrest that had been designated for it. Bruce and his colleagues needed to know whether a crime was an Arrestable Offence or not and what level of suspicion they needed before making an arrest. Reasonable suspicion was a crucial phrase and later Bruce would recall thinking what a subjective term this was. At the time, there was little discussion around the meaning of the terms. It was more like learning law much as children learned multiplication tables. At no point was the class asked to recite the list of Arrestable Offences in sing-song unison, but it was a close thing.

Linked to Powers of Arrest was the thorny subject known as Judges Rules. These were the conventions and processes that had evolved and become enshrined in a written code. They were so called because adherence to them meant that evidence, statements and police officers' pocket book notes would be admissible evidence in court. Mistakes or cutting corners would rule out potentially crucial and decisive evidence. The instructors stressed that allowing members of the criminal classes to get off on a technicality was the worst mistake a police officer could make. In sporting parlance, it amounted to an own goal, something to be avoided at all costs. With the benefit of hindsight Bruce would realize that the emphasis was on not wasting time and effort. There was no awareness of the importance of maintaining the purity of the justice process or of protecting the innocent. Irrespective of whether the true purpose of these guidelines was understood or not, their importance for pragmatic reasons was stressed at every opportunity.

Week by week Bruce and his colleagues sat at their desks, turning the bare facts of fictitious crimes committed in to pocket book entries followed quickly by statements for court. Their statements were set out according to a standard template and set in the fictional town called Blanktown; there was no place for purple passages of descriptive prose like the ones Bruce had memorized from Thomas Hardy novels in A-level English Literature. Statements were read aloud as each recruit took their turn in the witness box that was wheeled into the panelled classroom for simulated court sessions. One product of Eynsham Hall, schooled in this way, had announced himself on his first appearance in a real court as serving in Blanktown; such was the power of repetition!

There was no shortage of myths and rumours underpinning the culture of Eynsham. One of the most frequently discussed in late night conversations was the assertion that bromide was added to the tea and coffee in a bid to suppress the sex-drive of the virile young men corralled together in the Hall! When the lights went out at 10.30pm conversation would roam far and wide, taking in important topics such as politics, football, the size of Raquel Welch's breasts and the meaning of life. Pete Harmston was adamant he had inside information. He had spoken with one of the women on the kitchen staff.

"It's like in the army. They do it to avoid any funny business. I promise you they put it in on every day apart from Fridays." he said, one Thursday night in late October.

"Why don't they do it on Fridays?" asked "Norfolk".

"Come on don't be slow, Tractor Boy! Why do you think?" chipped in one of the Essex boys. "What do we all look forward to at the weekends – and I am not talking about Sunday lunch. You want to give the old lady or your bird a bit of prime English beef, don't yer."
"Too right, we do! And plenty of horseradish with it." The men were warming to the prospect of the coming weekend.

"I've told my missus I'll be Freddie Flintstone this weekend – giving it plenty of Yabba Dabba do!"

"More like plenty of Bam-Bam thank you Ma'am!" don't you mean." This was the contribution from the right honourable member for Bedfordshire!

"Anyway" he went on, "how does brimroid work?"

"It's bromide you pillock! I don't know. It must shrink your glands."

"If they are doing something to take the lead out of our pencils it's not fair. I've talked to my mate who's training at Ryton where they've got the women as well and he says some of them are at it like rabbits up there!" Norfolk was aggrieved to be missing out on the action.

Called into Question

"You really are thick ain't you!" Harmston's accent could sound very harsh at times. "They don't mind blokes doing the Wopsies. There's no room for poofters – that's what they're scared of, especially with Oxford being so close. Frightened those students might be a bad influence on us." The Londoner delivered this last sentence in a theatrical camp voice.

Bruce lay in the dark, not joining in the banter despite being stunned by the Londoner's logic. He almost said it was an infringement of their human rights but thought better of it. All the talk of sex left him subdued. He and Jenny had not had sex, or made love, as he preferred to think of it since the third weekend of the course – more than a month ago. Jenny lacked her normal energetic enthusiasm. She had said something about being tired from a run of night shifts. Bruce had put it down to them both adjusting to new routines. In the following weeks, there had been little opportunity for them to be alone. Once the nights started drawing in it was more difficult for young lovers. His Mini 1275 GT might handle well but it was hardly a passion wagon – far too cramped. Bruce thought back to the warm summer evenings and romantic walks along the banks of the Thames. The term the "playing fields of Eton" had taken on a new meaning for them that summer. He and Jenny had joked happily then about going to see their good friend Al Fresco! Bruce tried to dismiss any negative thoughts. They were both working hard. They would be ok once he had finished at Eynsham.

Stamina runs, weekly tests and practical sessions that included emergency midwifery helped the weeks slip by. November was a tough month. Any sense of novelty had worn off. The bright days of October had given way to colder, shorter dark days. Early morning parade was a rude awakening, freezing winds cutting through their uniforms as they awaited inspection. Bruce's marks in the weekly tests continued to set the standard for the class but lately he found himself increasingly distracted.

Bruce was looking forward to the last weekend in November. Jenny had the Friday through to Sunday night off. He was looking forward to some quality time together, perhaps a Saturday shopping expedition to Windsor, lunch in the Italian restaurant half-way down Castle Hill followed by the cinema in the evening. On the Sunday, he knew Jenny would want to join his family for lunch. His mother always did a special meal on Advent Sunday with small presents for each member of the family. He drove back that Friday feeling tired but more positive than he had for a while.
"I'm sorry Bruce. It's not fair of me to go on pretending! I can't help what I feel."

"But it's not what you feel is it? It's what you *don't* feel. That's what you are saying. Why? I don't get it? Why?"

They were sitting side by side, but not touching, on the edge of his bed. Bruce's shoulders were hunched. He was staring at the floor. When Jenny had turned down the trip to the cinema on the basis that they needed to talk, Bruce had immediately sensed a rising panic. They had gone up to his room and locked the door, for once with no trace of eager passion. She had not beaten about the bush – that was never her style. Her directness was one of the things that Bruce had first found attractive. She came straight out with it. "Bruce, I

Called into Question

am sorry but my feelings for you have changed. I can't go on looking ahead to a wedding when I feel like this. I am so sorry."

"You mean, finish, and break off our engagement? Jenny, you can't mean it. I love you. What about our plans?" Bruce felt he was reeling, winded as though he'd been hit by a truck.

"I know, I am so sorry. You will always be special to me, but something has changed for me." Jenny found it hard to meet his eye.

"What about my family? They love you too."

"I know they do and I love them. You are an amazing family but that's not enough Bruce. I have to love you and that's what's changed. I didn't expect it, I didn't plan it, but it has. I will go now. Do you want me to tell your mum?"

Bruce shook his head. "No, I will."

Jenny stood up. "I'll go then. Don't come down. Give me a hug."

They hugged, and Bruce was engulfed by a sob. He backed away.

"It wasn't meant to be like this Jen, not like this." She shut the door as she left. Bruce stood for a moment, threw himself on his bed and burying his face in the pillow surrendered to tears.

Chapter 4

December 3rd

£170 – quiet week. Lull before the Christmas rush. TC off for some winter sun, playing golf and Happy Families.

Clinic – ok, next appointment end of March.

Christmas card from Auntie Sally – enclosing a note from mum. Doesn't sound like she's decided, still unhappy but I can't deal with that, her fault not mine – her choice to believe him.

New copper on the patch – quiet, looks Asian, handsome and fit.

Chelsea Girl got some nice tops in their window – will wait for the sales, try and pick one up cheap.

Chapter 5

Bruce was not sure how he had got through his last two weeks at Eynsham Hall. For the first few days after the split he was numb, struggled to concentrate and felt like an automaton wading through the activities of the day. The Monday test after that fateful weekend with Jenny was the only one in which his score dipped below the 75% mark. At the end of the course this was to prove costly; he missed winning the Leading Student Award by two points. That honour went to a Cambridge graduate from the City of London force. However, Bruce did walk off with one prize. His stamina run times over the last two weeks improved. He ran like a man possessed, pushing himself so hard until it hurt. It was as though inflicting physical pain on himself gave relief, albeit temporarily from the emotional hurt.

His family members were shocked in their own way. Sarah and Hannah were tearful and repeatedly asked Bruce painful questions about why he and Jenny had split up. His parents offered sympathy, but Bruce detected an element of discreet relief. He knew that his parents and Jenny's had met to express their shared view that the young lovers were too immature to be making such a serious commitment to each other.

On the day of his Passing Out ceremony Bruce was acutely aware of the vacant seat beside his father as his parents watched from the rows of chairs overlooking the parade ground. He had a lump in his throat as they marched past the dignitaries to the accompaniment of *Colonel Bogey* played over ancient loud-speakers. He and his classmates would forever refer to this as "their tune" when they looked back on this brief but significant episode of their lives.

Bruce was expected to report for duty at Cheston Police Station on the Monday ten days before Christmas. He had been told some weeks before that, as a new arrival and therefore the lowest of the low, he would be working all over the Christmas period. In his present mood that suited him fine. The weekend between finishing at Eynsham Hall and starting work proper had been tense. Turning down a place in the Single Men's section house in favour of remaining with his family in the Manse had made good economic sense while he and Jenny were planning their future. Now it seemed not such a good idea. His parents' concern was obvious, and this annoyed Bruce. They would have been more concerned if they had known he began each day by swigging from a bottle of Lamb's rum hidden under his bed.

Things came to a head late on the Sunday afternoon. His sisters were listening to the chart show on Radio 1. *"It will be lonely this Christmas without you to hold"* by Mud had claimed top spot. Bruce stormed into their room. "Turn that bloody thing off before I smash it to pieces!"

The girls were stunned to see their normally controlled and composed big brother in a rage. They turned it off and looked sheepish. Bruce went back to his room, slammed the door and spent the rest of the evening away from the rest of his family. That wretched song would haunt him that Christmas and for many years to come.

The following morning, he drove into Cheston, parked his car correctly as instructed in the yard behind the station and made his way round to the front entrance of the modern red brick building. A stocky sergeant greeted him from behind the desk in the hallway. "Stand by everyone – Golden Boy arriving!" He pressed a button to release the reinforced glass doors that opened in to the main part of the station. "Come around to the front office PC Hammond."

Bruce felt embarrassed and irked to be greeted in that way. He tried not to let his discomfort show. He went into the office and was relieved that the Station Sergeant introduced him normally to the WPC and the Cadet who were sharing front office duties that day.

"Take a seat Hammond. I am Phil Fleming, Station Sergeant. The lovely Sandra will keep an eye on you. Don't believe everything she tells you, her old man is the only one who does that!"

"Thank you, Sarge – kind as ever!" Sandra was in her late twenties, a brunette with a friendly face. Bruce glanced at the wedding ring on her hand as she typed a charge sheet for a recently arrested prisoner. "Take no notice of him – we don't!" she said in a theatrical whisper. "This place is full of wind-up merchants. After a bit it's just water off a duck's back. The first half of the early shift will be in for their break around 9.30. I'll introduce you to Gareth Williams when he gets in. You'll be working with him for the first couple of weeks. He'll show you the ropes. He likes the mother hen role does our Gareth."

Called into Question

Gareth Williams was a quiet, kind but unambitious man who had been content to spend twenty years as a police constable. In his youth, he had followed relatives from South Wales who had trekked along the Great West Road a generation before and had settled in the area. He and his wife Lynne had no children. She doted on their spaniels while Gareth was devoted in equal measure to his allotment and the fortunes of the national rugby side. His life had a happy solidity to it.

Police officers do not carry L-plates round their necks when they are first released on to the streets. Bruce was grateful for the gentle steering hand of this wise, seasoned officer in that first fortnight. Gareth was a practical man. He sorted Bruce out with a locker, told him the code for the back door of the station, and explained the vagaries of the catering system in the canteen. These varied according to which shift they were on.

They walked Gareth's beat together and Bruce learned an important early lesson.
"Slow down, boyo!" At times Gareth's accent and expressions seemed exaggerated to the extent that Bruce thought he might be making fun of himself. "You move too fast, you've got to make the morning last!" Bruce was about to say he couldn't see any cobbled stones to kick when the older man went on. "If you hurry you will miss a lot of what's going on. Also, people will assume you are on your way to some incident and not come up to you to chatter. One of the best things we "Plods" can do is get a feel for what is happening on our patch. Even a quick conversation that appears to be little more than passing the time of day might turn out to be an important piece of a

jig-saw later."

Bruce could tell from the way all and sundry greeted Gareth, including many of the Asian shopkeepers, that he was working with a man who resembled Dixon of Dock Green, much loved of Bruce's childhood television viewing. Gareth gave Bruce his first lesson in cultivating tea spots, places where one could be assured of a quick cuppa and chat without going back to the police station for an official break. This was clearly an important part of a bobby's street craft. One afternoon in their second week of working together they were sitting in the back office of a launderette enjoying large mugs of sweet tea and mince pies courtesy of the owner, surrounded by baskets of washing.

Gareth looked thoughtful. "I wouldn't want to be starting out in the Force now. Don't get me wrong Bruce, I still think it's a grand job – but thing is, I know I am a bit of a dinosaur. I went on a day course last month. "Future of Policing" it was. Everything is going to get faster. They are looking for a leaner, fitter police service – working "smart and efficient" was what the bright spark from Bramshill called it. I know what that means though. They'll have you in a panda car before you know it. In theory, you'll have your helmet as well as your cap with you, so you can park and wander about, but it won't happen my son!"

Gareth broke off to have another mince pie. Bruce knew that Bramshill was the national police college where senior officers and younger men and women destined for high positions were trained. He hoped to go there in a couple of years, providing he did well in his sergeant's exams.

Called into Question

"You'll be racing around from job to job – no time to talk. Communications are getting quicker so everything else will follow. Have you been told about this here Police National Computer?" Gareth pronounced it as though it were a compooter! Bruce nodded. "Brilliant, for tracking stolen cars but it won't stop there. You mark my words now! We'll be leaner, but people will think we're meaner. Mind you it will all come full circle. Life's like that."

Bruce liked Gareth with his honesty and avuncular manner. He knew he himself was cut from different cloth but sensed this was wisdom he should not ignore. Gareth dunked the last piece of mince pie in his tea and deftly transferred it to his mouth. Swallowing it down, he completed his pep talk to his young temporary charge. "I know you are a bright lad Bruce and you might make a good copper in time. But you are going to have to be savvy and patient too. Cheston is not the easiest of nicks to work in. You'll get plenty of action, possibly more than you'll want. I have kept my head down and my mouth shut at times. I am happy with my life and unlike you I am not looking to change the world. I am telling you now, not to put you off, but to give you a heads up. There will be times when you will have to turn a blind eye to stuff you see. Understand?"

"Yes thanks. What sort of stuff are you talking about?"

"Ah, you'll see in good time boyo – be patient that's all I am saying. Your card is marked. That's a two-edged sword. Just be careful."

Called into Question

"Oh, come on Gareth, don't go all mysterious on me. You can't throw something like that out there and just leave it." Bruce leaned forward and looked the older man in the eye. "Give me a bit more to go on, please." Gareth thought for a moment. "You don't let up once you want something do you, young Hammond. I'll give you that. Ok, forget the official chains of command. The reality is that Cheston nick is bossed by CID. Detective Chief Inspector Ted Collins to be precise. If you think I am old school wait till you meet him. Proper old school but in a different way from me. The lads in CID call themselves "Teddy's Boys!" – think they are the Sweeney off the telly. Collins and Station Sergeant Phil Fleming did their National Service together, these days they golf together, go out on the razzle together and between them pretty much shape the way the whole show runs. They've got no time for the likes of you. They've already got their hooks into your pal Milkshake."

"Harpal, you mean!"

The Welshman raised an eyebrow. "Yep, whoever. Anyway, the word is Collins is on the look-out for you. Getting in the footie team has done you no favours. So, like I said, watch yourself."

With this Gareth stood up, brushed crumbs off his tunic and put on his helmet. Thanking their hostess, the two men left by the back door and made their way back on to the High Street via a side alley littered with beer cans, condoms and syringes.

The first Saturday of the new year was Bruce's first night shift out on the streets on his own. He felt self-conscious walking along, checking his reflection in shop windows every now and then to see whether his helmet was on straight. He was very aware of the dark hard wood truncheon in a concealed pocket. He could feel it knocking against his right leg just above his knee whenever he did as much as jog. Bruce suspected it would be an unwelcome impediment when the time came to give chase in earnest.

Just before 12.30am Bruce heard breaking glass and people shouting. Looking down the High Street he could see a scuffle involving half a dozen people taking place in the middle of the road outside the Cat Ballou nightclub. He started walking towards the fracas, reaching for his personal radio as he went.

"Kilo one-seven to base."

"Come in Kilo one-seven."

"Request back-up east end of High Street by Cat Ballou club. Fight taking place. Over."

"Roger Kilo one-seven. Message received."

As Bruce walked towards the trouble he heard the radio operator requesting mobile units to support him. His heart was racing despite his efforts to look calm. At Eynsham Hall they had been told by the instructors never to run to a fight. Officially this was to give time to make a cool assessment of what was happening. Unofficially it was to give the protagonists time to weaken each other thus making an arrest easier. Bruce was repeating the sergeant's words to himself "Never run to a fight!" as he battled the instinct to run. He was near enough to see that the argument was over a late-night taxi. The taxi's windscreen was shattered. The Asian driver was grappling with three youths while others were jeering and aiming clumsy kicks at the fighters from the sidelines. One of the young men had a bloodied nose. A teenage girl, presumably his girlfriend, was screaming hysterically.

Bruce could neither hear, nor see any sign of the support he had requested. Passing a queue at a bus stop thirty yards away from the trouble, a young woman shouted at him. "Oi copper, you should be running!"

As he reached the melee he was relieved to see the blue light of the Ford Transit van turn into the High Street. "All right everyone, calm down!" Bruce wanted to appear in command of the situation. He was surprised that his arrival signaled an abrupt end to hostilities. He felt a sense of satisfaction in not having run to the incident. He chuckled when he reflected on the girl at the bus stop and her advice. The sight of three other PCs and their Inspector had had the desired calming effect. It was unusual to see an Inspector out on the streets on a Saturday night, but Bob Middleton was not a typical Inspector. He led by example and was respected for that. He had a reputation for guarding his privacy. He rarely talked about his home life and family. Gareth had given Bruce a run-down on most of the senior officers as part of Bruce's induction. There had not been much to tell about Middleton. He was a Roman Catholic, married with four young children. Apparently, he was very involved in his church. He rarely mentioned his religion at work.

"So, what have we got here Hammond?"

"I've only just arrived myself, sir. Looks like an argument over a taxi got out of hand."

"Right. Get some names and addresses of witnesses. Gillespie and Fowlds, arrest those hot-heads and put them in the van." The Inspector turned to the taxi-driver who looked shaken and started to listen to his version of events. Fifteen minutes later, everyone had dispersed. The young men had been driven off to the station where they were charged with criminal damage and actual bodily harm. The onlookers drifted off comparing their versions of events as they went. The disconsolate taxi driver was left waiting for a mobile windscreen repairer to arrive. Bruce felt disappointed that he had been denied the chance to make his first arrest.

He did not have long to wait to get that first arrest under his belt, or more precisely on his Process Sheet. This was a large ring-binder at the station that contained a page for each officer on which they marked their tallies. These were collated monthly. Most shifts ran a sweepstake among themselves based on people's totals. When Gareth had showed him how to fill in the form Bruce had noticed that some PCs had significant numbers of arrests for Assault on Police and Drunk & Disorderly against their name.

Two nights after not having run to the fight Bruce lost his arresting virginity, as his colleagues called it. On night shifts in winter PCs on foot patrol were paired up with a Panda car for the second half of the night. Bruce had already discovered what it was like to have his breath freeze on his neat moustache on a cold night. He was grateful for this sensible concession. After his lunch break; a cheese and onion roll, a coffee and a game of snooker he joined Chris Fowlds in Panda 4. Chris had parked in a lay-by on the A4 heading out towards the motorway. Their conversation about the football results over the festive season was interrupted by an instruction to go to a phone box half a mile further down the road.

"Panda 4." It was the voice of Sergeant Phil Fleming. "We've got a bomb hoaxer on the line. We've traced the call to that phone box. Sandra is keeping him talking. Proceed quietly, try and catch him in the act and nick him."

"Roger, Sarge. Closing in now. Panda 4 over and out."
Chris brought the car to a gentle halt. He parked where the caller could not see them through the solid back panel of the call box.

"Ok Bruce. We'll walk up quietly. Listen to him enough to confirm he's making the call and then you nick him. Alright?"

Bruce nodded. They could hear the caller clearly. He had a heavy almost comical Irish accent. Chris signalled to Bruce. They moved swiftly round opposite sides of the box. Chris snatched the door open.
"All right laddy. Time to ring off I think!"

The caller was a weedy looking teenager, sixteen or seventeen at the most. He was so startled that he dropped the handset which swung round and round

Called into Question

uncoiling itself like a snake. The young man pressed himself into the corner of the tiny booth. "I'm sorry, I'm sorry." All trace of the Emerald Isle had vanished from his voice, replaced by pathetic pleading fear.

Chris put the receiver to his ear. "Ok we've got him. Confirm time as 12.50am and that you WPC Sutton were on the line taking this call." He stepped out of the call box. The young lad was sitting on the floor, hunched over his knees, his head in his hands. He began to cry and rock slightly back and forwards.

"Ok PC Hammond, find out his name, read the caution and arrest him for wasting police time under section 5 of the Criminal Law Act 1967." Bruce was impressed at the detail. "I had one like this last month – bleeding nuisance!" Chris explained.

Bruce put his arm on the young man's shoulder. "Come on stand up and stop crying. We're not going to hurt you. Now what's your name?"

The lad did as he was told. "It's Peter, Peter Larkins." he snivelled.

"How old are you Peter and where do you live?" Bruce asked as kindly as he could.

"I'm seventeen. I used to live at Cedar Lodge but I'm in a bed-sit now." Bruce knew that Cedar Lodge was a residential unit for young people with learning difficulties. His father had led a carol service there a few years ago.

"Is there anyone you want us to ring?" The miserable lad shook his head.

"Ok. Listen to me. Peter Larkins, I am arresting you for Wasting Police Time under section 5 of the Criminal Law Act 1967. You are not obliged to say anything, but anything you do say may be taken down and used in evidence against you in a court of law. Do you have anything to say?" A shake of the head and a sniffle.

"The accused gave no answer." Bruce looked across at his colleague to check he'd done all the necessary.

"Right then. Let's get him back down the nick. It'll be a damn sight warmer than here. Put him in the back and get in with him."

They walked back to the car and Bruce guided him in to the back seat. Chris radioed in. "Panda 4."

"Panda 4 go ahead."

"Young male arrested. On our way now. Two teas one with, one without. Cheers."

"Message received Panda 4."

Sergeant Fleming was waiting at the rear entrance. "Ok you can push off now Fowlds. Hammond, you process him."

Called into Question

"Yes Sarge."

Bruce typed a charge sheet, finger-printed the prisoner, taking his time as the Sergeant watched. Then the Sergeant read the charge sheet, repeated the caution that Bruce had given at the time of arrest and took a handful of small change and a key from the young man.

"You'll get those back later. Now let's get you down the cell and give both you youngsters a lesson." Bruce was puzzled by the choice of words.

The Sergeant led the way. Bruce followed behind Peter Larkins as they went through a large metal grill to the corridor of cells. There were five each side. The thick doors were painted duck egg blue with a peep hole and sliding cover on the outside.

"Take your shoes and your belt off and leave them outside." Larkins did as he was told. The corridor smelled like a toilet block. The air was heavy with the fetid smell of feet, body odour and urine. Bruce sensed the young man had withdrawn into himself. He noticed that the Sergeant had a pair of leather driving gloves in his hand, black with a bright stud on each.

"In you go, you pathetic waste of space you!" The sergeant gave him a hard shove as he went through the door. Larkins stumbled from the force of the push.
"Come in Hammond and stand in the middle of the cell. You, thicko! Stand facing the wall there." The young man turned to the wall. Bruce felt

increasingly uncomfortable.

"Right Hammond. An important lesson." He fixed Bruce in the eye. "We are not enforcing the law here, we are not upholding the law or any other fancy word you want to choose. We are the bloody law. So, let me show you how we do things round here." He turned back towards the cowering youth.

"And sonny boy, the law does not take kindly to having its' time wasted. Do you understand?"

Larkins nodded.

"I said, do you understand?" Leaving no time for a reply he raised the gloves which he was holding by the fingers and lashed them with a powerful backhand movement against the side of the youth's face.

"Hey!" He moved a side step. The sergeant moved in and struck again.

"Keep your hands down, you disgusting piece of shit." Bruce flinched as he watched. "Don't you dare waste our time again. Do you understand?" Fleming struck the lad half a dozen more times as he retreated round the walls of the cell. Bruce could see there were red welts all over his face. Blood was oozing from a nick above his right eye. Peter Larkins began to sob.

"Right let that be a lesson to you both, that's how we work round here. Hammond give him some water and then lock him in overnight."

Bruce was relieved to see Fleming leave the cell. This was surreal. He stood for what seemed an age. He looked down at his first arrest. He was cowering in the corner, rocking and sucking his thumb. If this was losing "his arresting virginity", it felt like rape. "I'll bring you some water. I'm sorry."

Chapter 6

"What I can't get out of my head is the thought that I should have done something. I mean, I just stood there watching. I never said a thing."

"It's no good beating yourself up over it. Sorry, not good choice of words. You said you apologized to the lad and were kind to him. I don't think you could do more than that."

Being on different shifts the two men did not get many opportunities to socialize together and to compare experiences. Bruce had a day off and Harpal had been on early turn. They had arranged to play squash in the afternoon at the local sports centre. They were well-matched. Bruce needed to use his length of reach and natural athleticism to compensate for his inferior court craft. Harpal played squash as though he were playing chess, all boasts and feints he plotted his way through rallies moving the taller man around the court at will. On this occasion, he got the better of Bruce over five hard-fought games.

As they stood toweling themselves dry by the showers Bruce could not help but admire his friend's physique. Not lacking in physical confidence himself, he recognized that Harpal possessed a grace, which he imagined would, appeal greatly to women. The effortless way he moved around the squash court reflected a wider sense of balance and of being in control.

"It didn't feel like enough. Obviously, it was for my benefit but it's like, I don't know, I feel compromised already. What's that saying, "The only thing necessary for the triumph of evil is for good men to do nothing?"

Harpal nodded "Edmund Burke, allegedly. It's a fine saying and is true but Bruce, be realistic we are not going to change things from the bottom of the pile. We have to be patient."

"I guess so, but I wonder how many others before us have thought that they could change things once they were more senior? By the time they get there they've become part of the system themselves."

"You haven't met DCI Collins yet have you?" asked Harpal.

Bruce shook his head.

"I went up to CID last week to hear about my placement with them. Collins was there in his office. He saw me through his open door. He called out, "Goodness gracious me, is that a snake charmer I see before me?" All his cronies thought this very funny. They are a bunch of creeps. He called me into his office. "Shut the door Shaik. So, what are you then? A charmer or a snake? Or maybe both.""

"Blimey, what did you say?"

"Nothing. He was looking for a reaction. I wasn't going to give him one.

Anyway, he basically said I wasn't welcome in the nick but, seeing as they had to have me, I might be useful as a secret weapon against all the cheating Pakkis taking over the town. Now that winds me up."

"What does?" asked Bruce, pulling a sweatshirt over his head.

"Being called a Pakki. It's so ignorant. It's like calling a proud Welshman like Gareth, French! I don't think I've met anyone in this country who has even the faintest idea of the history of the Indian sub-continent. And yet you Brits had such an impact in shaping it."

Bruce thought back to history lessons at school. He vaguely remembered learning about Clive of India and the East Indian Company and its' private army but knew he would be hard-pressed to come up with dates and details. Partition and the struggle for independence were never mentioned.

"When are you starting your CID placement?"

"In a couple of weeks. It will be alright. I'll keep you posted. I'll tell you what. Collins is a West Ham fan. He's got a scarf draped over a framed picture of him shaking hands with Bobby Moore. So, no wonder he's got all the charm and logic of Alf Garnett. What sort of people watch that rubbish, that's what I'd like to know? Now I think you are buying the teas, loser!"

Bruce felt embarrassed remembering how in his mid-teens he loved staying up with his dad watching the Saturday night double-header of "*Till death us do part*" and *Match of the Day*. "I think it is meant to be satirical, but I suspect

Called into Question 54

lots of people don't get it."

"Well our friend DCI Collins certainly doesn't see it that way. As far as he's concerned Alf Garnett is the voice of reason, spokesman for the common man. Come on, a cuppa and an Eccles cake for me please."

Over tea in the café they shared their experiences of the early weeks at Cheston. In keeping with Bruce's first impressions of him, Harpal Shaik was very philosophical and calm about the challenges that faced them. Bruce wondered if this was a direct result of his Hindu beliefs. He wanted to open up the subject of faith and family background. However, something in him acted as a check. His own beliefs were in a state of flux and this held him back. He knew that his friend would turn any question he asked back on him, not out of any awkwardness but out of genuine interest.

Harpal was in the middle of telling Bruce about how his uncle had introduced him to squash at an early age at the Parklands Sports Club in Nairobi when he was suddenly distracted.

"Check her out, the slim blonde in the tight bell-bottoms."

"Where?" asked Bruce, not wanting to miss out.

"There, just going into the women's changing rooms." Harpal gestured with his head.

Bruce followed his gaze. "Mmm! Long legs and nice bum. I didn't see her face though. Face is always the clincher. I remember being shocked when my dad told me it's the face the matters. His actual words were "No good if you have to put a sack over their head". It seemed so out of character."

"Your dad doesn't sound like a typical minister."

"No, I guess he isn't. Talking of parents, do your folks know you've got a thing about pretty white girls?"

"Who says I have?" asked Harpal indignantly.

"Come on. It's obvious. You just spotted the bird over there and the first time we spoke you were drooling over a girl at Tramps."

"I'm only window shopping. No harm in that."

"Are you telling me you wouldn't actually go out with a white girl?"
Harpal hesitated. "I didn't say that. Just that my parents would go ballistic if they found out I was dating a gori."

"A gori? What's that?"

"Sorry, it's slang for a white girl dating an Asian man."

"There you go. I learn something new every day."

Called into Question

"Listen Bruce, if we are going to hang out together a bit more, remember not to blurt stuff out about girls to my family, okay?"

"Yeah, sure. No problem. But is there someone at the moment?"

"That would be telling. All in good time my friend, all in good time. When are you playing your first match for the force?"

"Ha, subtle change of subject! Next week, Wednesday afternoon, a so-called friendly against the Met at Maidenhead United's ground. Fancy coming? Should be a bit tasty I imagine."

"Yeah may do, day-off that day. I'll let you know."

The following Wednesday, Bruce was grateful for his friend's presence at the game. He knew Harpal was not much of a football fan. The game itself went well for Bruce. As predicted it was a hard-fought affair with no quarter given from either side. Metropolitan Police officers had a reputation for patronizing their provincial cousins and they missed no opportunity to remind other forces of their superiority. Their football squad was no exception. There was no shortage of sharp and illegal tackles. The referee had his work cut out to spot clashes off the ball.

Bruce was playing centre-forward and was being marked by a burly ginger-haired man in his mid-thirties. His breath smelt of tobacco and curry. Early in the game they were side by side waiting for a corner kick to be taken.

Called into Question

"So, what's a nice boy like you doing playing with the grown-ups?" Bruce did not rise to the bait. "My sources tell me, you've got no mates in this team, so you'd better look out for yourself. hadn't you? You dago-looking ponce you." The man's ability to insult and offend was matched by neither speed of thought nor fleetness of foot. By contrast Bruce, who was now not lacking in motivation, felt sharp and fit. He got the better of his marker on a regular basis, scored two goals and set-up another. The match ended in a three-all draw which, given recent history between the two, represented a feather in his force's cap. At the end of the match two of his team mates offered grudging appreciation of his efforts. However, this did not extend to including Bruce in the post-match drinking session at a local pub.

"Well played the wonder boy!" exclaimed Harpal waiting by Bruce's car.

Bruce winced. "Don't talk like that. I get enough of that crap without you joining in."

"Sorry. Anyway, well played, impressive."

"Cheers. And thanks for coming – really appreciate it."

"No problem. You know what we said. The outsiders have got to stick together."

A few weeks later Bruce was on night shift, seven nights in a row. Other PCs had told him how good nights were in summer, pleasant to be out and about on warm evenings with the possibility of not going to bed the following day. Bruce was unconvinced. For the time being these nights early in the year were cold and, weekends apart, often far too quiet. Once the pubs shut there were long stretches of the night with little to do, even when paired up in a patrol car. Bruce's thoughts would still, unless he was very careful, revisit painful memories of his split with Jenny. He wondered how she was doing. Although she had promised not to become a stranger they had had little contact. He was left guessing what she was up to and this was far more of a torment.

By now he had got to know the back alleys and service entrances to the stores on the High Street. Week by week he discovered aspects of the town which he had never known despite living in the area for a few years. He was not due back to the station for another hour. He decided to walk round behind the parade of shops at the far end opposite the night club. The 1950's complex housed a launderette, a book-makers and a Chinese take-away. The back of these shops was a winning pick for anyone looking for a warm spot. Bruce had become acquainted with the owner of the take-away. A discreet tap on the back door usually resulted in a free bag of chips or a couple of spring rolls. Chinese take-away chips always tasted different from British chippy ones! Bruce assumed they must use different types of oil.

He was sitting on a large rubbish bin in the shadows behind the shop when he heard the unmistakable sound of high heels crunching on the loose surface of the service road. A tall, slim girl turned the corner only to freeze with shock at the sight of Bruce enjoying his chips. She was not dressed to keep out the cold. White patent boots, a quartered black and white miniskirt, a tight black blouse and a short black shiny coat were topped off with a matching "Donny Osmond" cap. Bruce's gaze was drawn to her slender shapely legs. He had found himself strangely appreciative of black fishnet tights ever since his grandmother had declared during a *Carry On* film that only French tarts wore them. Even in the half-light Bruce could see the girl was heavily made up. She looked like a frightened rabbit caught in headlights. "Oh sorry. I didn't know you were here. I'll go." She turned to go.

"It's alright. You don't need to go. I'll be gone in a bit. There's no reason for you to have known I'd be here." Bruce said gently.

The girl hesitated.

"Here, have some chips. I'll never manage all these."

"Are you sure?" Her voice was more cultured than he had expected. Bruce could see that despite long false eyelashes and heavy eye make-up she had fine features.

Bruce shifted on the bin to make room for her. She sat down. Her scent was strong and musky. For a moment, there was an awkward silence. Bruce reflected on the irony of the situation. He could not help wondering what would happen if his sergeant suddenly appeared to check up on him. Would he be congratulated on making another good contact? Or would he be reprimanded for his naivety? Either way he suspected there would be jealousy involved.

"You're new, aren't you?" The girl broke the silence.

"Yes, started just before Christmas."

"Thought so. I've seen you going up and down the High Street. You're still checking your reflection in the shop windows." Bruce felt embarrassed on two counts. Being caught out in his moments of vanity annoyed him but he was more disappointed with himself for not having noticed this regular on his beat. He felt himself unnerved by this girl, frustrated by his inability to read her.

"I'm Bruce, Bruce Hammond." The girl nodded and having taken another mouthful of chips was unable to reciprocate with her name.

Bruce waited. "And you are…?"

She hesitated. Resting her hands on the edge of the bin, she looked sideways at Bruce, weighing him up.

"You can call me Holly." she said, nodding her head as though responding to her own internal question.

"Holly what?" Bruce regretted the supplementary question almost before it was out. He noticed her stiffen, an almost involuntary shiver like a young horse about to bolt.

"I said, Holly. That'll do. Thanks for the chips. I'll be off now."

Called into Question

"Ok. See you around." He watched her retreating figure. She seemed familiar. She raised a hand and without turning gave a hint of a wave.

Returning to the station at the end of the shift Bruce picked up a pre-carboned triplicate report form. The top white copy went to the shift sergeant, the yellow copy went in the first instance to the Collator's office, where all intelligence and information was sifted and stored, the officer kept the final pink one for his own records. Sitting at the large table in the shift room surrounded by grey metal lockers Bruce reflected on the evening. He was surprised to find himself hesitating to include any reference to his meeting with Holly. He wrote a long paragraph about the lack of security on the new bus station building site. It was an accident waiting to happen with heavy plant and valuable equipment left wherever the predominantly Irish navvies had downed tools at the end of their shift. Bruce told himself he would wait until he had rather more information to offer about the mysterious Holly.

Chapter 7

February 4th

£280 – good. No wonder I'm tired.

My room is cold – scrounged extra blankets from Lisa across the hall.

Splashed out on a sketch book, don't feel inspired though. Bought charcoal – messy.

Finally met the other new copper called Bruce, introduced himself – bit wet, he'll learn. He asks lots of questions. Prefer the Asian one, mysterious. Looks like they've palled up – saw them at the Sports Centre.

Letter from Auntie Sally - still trying to persuade me to change my mind. Hope she keeps her promise. I think she will.

Chapter 8

Young police officers grew up fast in Cheston. Winter became spring, marked by splashes of crocuses along the edge of the dual carriage-ways and daffodils in the park. Bruce felt himself growing in confidence. One of the attractions of the police, apart from the sport and promise of a house, had been the expectation that each day would be different. He was meeting a wide variety of local characters. He had cultivated a tea spot at the local sex shop. Known as the Honey Pot it was run by a cheerful Irish woman in her mid-fifties. Once a week Bruce would sit with her in the back-office peering through the garish plastic strip blinds as men grubbed through the wares on offer. The manageress, as she liked to be known, whispered hilarious observations to Bruce. "Ha, now look at him would you. He doesn't need to be buying one of them! For sure, a glass of whisky and a firm grasp would sort out his problem." Until this point Bruce's sex education, had consisted of some boring pamphlets from his mother, a belated chat from his father and an over-technical lecture from the biology teacher in the second year at school. He and Jenny had managed well enough. Some items in the shop were exotic eye-openers but he saw nothing that he could imagine ever wanting to buy for a future girlfriend. Occasionally after his cuppa in the Honey Pot he made discreet notes when he spotted known flashers spending time there.

There was light relief and moments of comedy scattered throughout the weeks. On a couple of occasions Bruce found himself the butt of practical jokes by members of the public. The first time he was caught out it was by students from the local college. A pretty girl emerged one day from a laughing group carrying a handbag. "Please officer," she said smiling coyly, "we've found this bag. It's got a pound note in, so we thought we should hand it in to you. I can't take it to the station cos we're about to go into lectures." Bruce looked at the old cheap bag. Inside there was indeed a one-pound note and a piece of paper. The students ran off whooping with delight. Bruce unfolded the paper. It read, "Handbag suits you, big poofter!!" He radioed for a panda car to come and pick it up, but none came. He was forced to hold onto it until his tea break. He attracted sniggers as he walked back with it under his arm. It came as no surprise to be greeted by the sergeant and other members of the shift. The sergeant had the Instamatic camera from the charge room to hand to capture Bruce's embarrassment.

The second such incident had not been planned but turned out to be equally embarrassing. One afternoon a young man came running out from a block of offices. "Quick, there's a dog loose on the dual carriageway. We saw it from our office up there." Fifty yards or so down the road a brindle, frightened mongrel was running in and out of the traffic. Most drivers were slowing down but a few were unhelpfully hooting their horns scaring the dog even more. Bruce started to run towards the animal, after all this time it was not a fight he thought to himself. "Can you get me some string or something from your office?" he called to the public-spirited clerk. It was an order more than a question. One or two passers-by had gathered on the pavement. "Anyone got anything like a biscuit I can use to attract it?"

"I've got some chicken livers." piped up a black woman. "Give her one of these, sweetheart." she said, unwrapping a package from her large raffia

Called into Question

shopping bag.

"Thanks." Bruce held out the tit-bit which worked a treat. The scrawny dog came over to him at once. She had whelped recently and looked in need of food and attention. Bruce grasped her neck, slightly anxious that she would give him a nip. He stroked her chest with his other hand. She calmed visibly. At this point the young man from the office appeared with a length of parcel twine. Bruce looped it securely round the dog.

"Well done young man." said the cheery liver donor. His sense of satisfaction did not last long, quickly replaced by the realization that he would have to walk the dog back to the police station himself. The handbag episode had taught him not to expect much by way of back-up in situations like this. Walking down the High Street with the dog alongside he sensed people's amusement. A taxi driver waiting at traffic lights wound his window down. "Blimey, government cuts are getting bad if police dogs have been down-graded." As he expected, again there was a welcoming committee awaiting him at the station.

By now the banter Bruce took from his colleagues on the shift was no more than normal for a bunch of men working together. In fact, he took it as a sign of acceptance and gave as good as he got. He more than held his own in the snooker games they played during meal breaks. A modest amount of money changed hands on the outcome of a frame or two. When they were on a week of nights one of the shift organized a sweepstake called the Not-so-Grand National. This was a series of races that they held in the new shopping precinct near the bus station. Members of the shift paired up. One would sit in a shopping trolley with his legs curled up looking like a garden gnome. The other provided the motive force much like a member of a bob-sleigh team. Bruce was too tall to fit in a trolley so used his running speed and fitness to good effect. One week, he and his partner made over a tenner in winnings.

At the end of March Bruce was pleasantly surprised to discover that Harpal was being moved on to his shift. His friend told him the news on one of their trips to the sports centre. "It's because two others are transferring. One has been made up to Sergeant and the other is moving to CID in Maidenhead. It will make fixing squash easier."

"Great. I suppose it also makes it easier for the boys upstairs to keep an eye on us. I heard one of them call us Butch Cassidy and the Sundance Kid the other day." said Bruce.

"No prize for guessing which I am then is there?" Harpal smiled. "Look, there's that girl again – check that bum out! Oof, I wouldn't mind cupping hands round that on a dance floor."

Bruce followed Harpal's gaze. "I know her!"

"You know her!" Harpal exclaimed. "How come?"

"Um, she works, I mean I've seen her on my beat once or twice. Her name is Holly."

"If I was a lawyer questioning you in court I would jump on an answer like that and press hard, very hard. Very unconvincing. I put it to you officer that you are withholding something from the court. Come on Bruce what do you mean she works on your patch?"

Bruce hesitated. "Ok. Sorry. She works as a tart. I met her a few weeks ago."

"A tart? What you mean an actual pro? She doesn't look like a tart at all. Are you sure?"

"Yes, I am. But obviously she isn't your typical prostitute. She has what I guess she'd call her work outfit, but even that's quite classy. She's on her own, keeps away from the slappers on the edge of the trading estate."

"Have you mentioned her in your reports?" asked Harpal.

"No, not yet. I thought I would try and get to know her a bit more first." Bruce was acutely aware of how unconvincing that sounded.

Harpal grinned at him. "Well, be careful. No under the covers work with that one."

"Thanks for the advice Chief Constable Shaik! Now that has a certain ring to it!"

"Ha dream on, my friend. It will be a very long time before a non-white reaches that sort of rank."

Called into Question

"Do you think a woman will make it first?"

"Ooh, tough one to call." Harpal whistled through his teeth. "I wouldn't hold your breath on either if I were you."

"Anyway, going back to Holly. I've got my CID placement next month, so you'll have to wait for the next installment on that front."

Although he knew he would come in for some abuse Bruce was looking forward to his month attached to CID. Having grown up, like most young men, on a TV diet of sport and assorted crime series he fancied the idea of a career as a detective. He hoped his powers of observation coupled with his ability to think through a range of possibilities would serve him well.

Going into work in plain clothes and working to a more flexible shift pattern was a novelty to Bruce. He enjoyed the variety of the work and found that time on duty flew past more quickly than when walking his beat. He did not have to endure the sort of abusive welcome from DCI Collins that Harpal Shaik had been subjected to.
At the end of the first week he was on mobile patrol with a Detective Constable called Rob Finlay, generally known as Finn. They were driving towards the railway station in their red Ford Escort when Finn pointed out a group of six black youths walking ahead of them. The youths who looked in their mid-teens were laughing and joking as they walked. One of them in the middle was swinging a sports bag above his head.

Finn slowed the car and gestured to Bruce to lower the nearside window. The gang members had not noticed them and were taken by surprise when the car drew up alongside.

Finlay leaned across Bruce. "Afternoon lads, on our way to catch a train, are we?"

"Yeah man we're going up Southall for some action."

"What sort of action is that then? Music, screw a few honeys, do some drugs?" Finn asked casually. "What's in the bag then?" Bruce noticed that whoever had been carrying the black Puma sports bag had dropped it on to the pavement. The teenagers looked at it in mock surprise as though it had just landed among them from outer space.

"Nothing!" The shortest member of the gang made up for his lack of height by acting as spokesman for the group.

"Well if it's nothing, you won't mind if I get out and check for myself will you." Finn opened his door as he spoke.

"Aw, come on man. Don't hassle us. It's nothing. Just some bottles of Red Stripe and cassettes."

"Red Stripe eh. Good, I do like a drop of that in an afternoon. Save me going down the ACC to get some. They should brew this over here. You been down the old ACC yet Hammond?"

Bruce looked at him blankly.

"The Afro-Caribbean Club man! It's cool. You should come down. Teach you to dance to reggae proper like." The spokesman and the other gang members were obviously relaxing. Bruce guessed this was Finn's ploy.

Suddenly Finn grabbed the bag. Before he could unzip it, the youths all made a break in different directions as though a starting pistol had been fired.

"Quick, stop one of them!"

Bruce looked around and set off after one of the group who had headed towards the station. Despite the head-start Bruce quickly made up ground on him. "Stop or I'll take you down." Bruce was right on his shoulder now. The youth hesitated, weighing his options before coming to a halt.

"Sensible choice. Come back with me. And don't even think about making another dash for it." Bruce put one hand on the young man's back and went to hold him near the wrist with the other.

"Don't touch me man." The youth jerked his arm from Bruce's grasp. "I won't run. But just don't touch me ok?"

"Calm down." Bruce walked back with him to the car where DC Finlay was standing with the sports bag at his feet, holding a plastic wrap of what looked like old grass trimmings in his hand.

"Nice work Bruce, you are bloody quick aren't you. Now then sunshine, your friends seem to have disappeared."

The young man stood looking at the ground, his hands in his pockets trying to look relaxed.

"Look at me." Finn's tone was now sharp and aggressive. "So, whose marijuana is this? It was rolled up inside an empty bottle."

The young man looked the detective in the eye. "It isn't mine. I didn't even know it was there."

"I didn't ask if it was yours did I." The DC was becoming angry. "I asked whose it was. Who does this bag belong to?" Finn kicked the bag as he spoke.

"I don't know. I'm not sure." The youth looked miserable, all trace of casualness gone. He sounded scared.

"So, you really don't know which of your absent friends owns this bag? You haven't got a name to give me." Finn asked dropping his voice.

"No. I told you man."

"Well it is very impressive not grassing up your mates- excuse the pun, won't you? Unfortunately for you it means I can only come to one conclusion." He paused for effect. "And that is – this bag must belong to you!"

Called into Question

"No way man, no way. I told you it's not mine!"

Finn stuck his face forward, so he was just inches from the frightened youth. "I told you I think it's yours. And what is more PC Hammond and I both saw you carrying it as we approached. Didn't we Hammond?" It was Bruce's turn to be surprised. Finlay left no space for a reply. "And I have a feeling that the magistrates are more likely to believe the word of two police officers over the stammering of a skinny black boy. What do you say now? Are you sure you haven't remembered a name?"

"You're joking right. You can't do this! No way. You're mad. Like you're expecting me to say - Yeah, sorry. It's my bag, my hash and I was here on my own!" The black youngster was now outraged. Bruce readied himself for another chase.

"We'll see, won't we? You heard him PC Hammond, I don't think we need to waste any more time here. Now do we need to handcuff you or are you going to behave? Put him in the back and snuggle in alongside Hammond."

Driving back to the station Bruce's mind was racing. He could not believe what he had witnessed. The young man sat still looking out of the window. This was one of the most awkward silences Bruce had ever experienced. Arriving at the back-entrance DC Finlay led the unfortunate youth to an interview room.

"I'll sort out the charge papers and process with Sergeant Fleming." He nodded towards the sports bag and its' dubious contents in the front passenger foot well. "Take that into forensics and get it labeled. If they ask, tell them we're doing the guy for Possession of a Class B drug under the '71 Misuse of Drugs act. They'll be fine with that. I'll bring a case number up later."

Bruce took the bag up to the small office adjacent to the main CID team office and set about labeling it as he had been shown when starting the placement. He went over to the drinks cupboard and made himself a black instant coffee. It tasted bitter. He reached for the thick glass ash tray that passed for a sugar bowl. All that was left was a disgusting crystallized ring where people had left wet spoons.

When DC Finlay came up about half an hour later he beckoned Bruce over to join him at his desk.

"Right, I'll sort out your statement for you. And then we can fix our pocket books. Kind, aren't I?"

Bruce took a deep breath. By now, he had had a chance to rehearse what he would say. He tried to keep his voice even and controlled. "Finn, are you seriously going to pin this on that lad? We don't have a clue whose bag and stuff that really is. We didn't even caution him when we nicked him."

Finn looked at Bruce for a few seconds. Then he lit himself a cigarette, put his feet on his desk and brushed a speck of ash off his brown desert boots. There was a tide mark of white sediment along the sides.

"Listen Hammond. This is my arrest; my case and I am not having you screw it up. Understood? You are on placement to learn how we work. So, you will bloody well shut up and do as you are told. Got it?"

Bruce stared back. He sensed there was more to come.

"Don't even think about spouting off about Judges' Rules, Cautions and all that crap you heard at Eynsham. That's just hoops to jump through – like the stuff you do when you are learning to drive. Mirror, signal, manouevre – once you pass your test you dump it. We will write out our pocket books and that becomes the reality – that's what happened. Right? Now I distinctly heard our young black friend admit it was his bag and his drugs."

"Finn, he was being sarcastic – that wasn't a confession."

"I've got news for you, smart arse. If you and I both write down more or less the same version, the court won't pick up on subtle tones and they certainly aren't going to believe him. I will type out our statements. Make sure your pocket-book matches what I write. All you have to remember is, when asked if you made notes as soon as possible at the time, to say it is a close record of what happened."

"Sorry. There is no way I can stand in court and swear to a bunch of lies."

"You can't? Well, let me tell you Lady La-di-pissing-dada you are going to have to explain yourself to DCI Collins when he comes back from leave next week. I have a feeling he won't be over-impressed."

Bruce was grateful to have the following weekend off. He decided that for the time being discretion was the better part of valour. He had written minimal notes in his pocket-book and left Finn to write the statements. He hoped he would get a chance to have a quiet word with either Harpal or Gareth before facing DCI Collins. A weekend of home comforts was a welcome prospect.

Chapter 9

April 7th

£225 – good run.

Test results back – clear, feel relieved.

Got bus down to Eton over one lunch time. Eton boys look such prats in their uniform – got a few whistles and shouts off some older ones.

Walked over the bridge and along the river. Did some sketches – feels good, million miles away from work.

TC - his usual. Wants me to do him a favour, eyes and ears.

Chapter 10

Bruce tried to make the most of the weekend and kept his inner turmoil under control. On Saturday afternoon, he cut The Manse lawn. There was something reassuring about the smell of freshly-cut grass. The neat stripes were pleasing on the eye and gave the illusion of an ordered world.

He had arranged to play squash with Harpal on Sunday. The opportunity to talk through the events of the previous week would be a great relief. He was also looking forward to losing himself in the physical effort of a keenly-contested match. So, he was particularly disappointed when his friend rang on Saturday evening to say that he would not be able to play. Apparently, his parents had arranged for him to meet some guests. Harpal had been reluctant to elaborate.

On Sunday afternoon Bruce decided not to waste the booking he had made. It gave him the chance for some practice. He put himself through a set of punishing drills: ten shots close to the forehand wall, ten down the backhand wall and then a series of side-wall boasts, followed by a drop-shot finishing with a lob in to the back corner of the court. It was an impressive effort. Bruce pushed himself hard. He wanted it to hurt.

"God, you're fit aren't you." The words startled him as he stood on the red T marking at the centre of the court gasping. He looked up to the viewing gallery at the back of the court. He had been unaware that he was being watched. He had no idea how long Holly had been there, such had been the intensity of his concentration. She was wearing a light-blue hooded sweat shirt and dark blue tracksuit bottoms.

"Do you fancy a knock up?" Bruce called up, his words echoing in the court.

"Pardon?" Holly looked surprised. "What did you say?"

Bruce could feel himself blushing. He had blurted out the question on impulse. "Do you want to come down and hit a few shots?"

"I don't have a racket." Holly replied. Bruce had expected her to say that she did not know how to play.

"That's ok. I have my spare here." Bruce always left his second racket with his valuables under a towel against the tin at the front of the court. He prepared for all eventualities and losing a match due to a broken string was never on his agenda.
He could see Holly weighing up his offer. As ever, she was hesitant. He could almost hear the "cogs" whirring in her racing mind.

"You sure that would be alright?" she asked eventually.

"Yeah! Why not? Just a few shots. No-one's going to watch us." He guessed that fear of being seen playing with a police officer was at the root of her uncertainty.

"Come down, as long as the soles of your shoes aren't going to mark the floor."

Holly lifted one foot and glanced down to check. "I think they're ok. They're white. Alright I'll come down." She smiled and turned towards the stairs down from the gallery.

It was soon apparent that Holly was no novice. She dispatched a couple of Bruce's lazy shots to the backhand corner of the court. He struggled to make a return. He started to put a little more effort in to his play and found himself admiring Holly's poise and balance, and the pleasing view of her rear as she moved around the court. He was embarrassed and slightly ashamed to find himself thinking, *"I am getting hot and sweaty in a squash court with a prostitute whom I find attractive."*

They decided to call it a day. "Well you've obviously played before. Where was that?"

Holly had enjoyed their rallies and was glowing from the effort and the pleasure. She handed back Bruce's racket. "We had courts at one of my schools. I played some of the guys when we were in the 6th form." Holly stopped suddenly and looked down at the floor. "I had better be off now. Thanks for asking me. I liked that."

"Don't rush off. Have a cup of tea. I'm at a loose end and would appreciate the company."

For the second time that afternoon Bruce could see Holly deliberating, weighing up her options, calculating the risks. He sensed she needed some form of reassurance. His intuition was spot on.

"Look, Harpal bombed me out – that's why I was practicing on my own. I'm not coming on to you and I'm not in work mode."

"What about the "a good copper is never off-duty" line?" Holly looked Bruce in the eye.

"Fair enough, but perhaps I'm not a good copper. I'm simply being friendly, but I understand. I won't take it personally."

Something about him convinced Holly. "Sorry. I didn't mean to be rude. Force of habit, I'm afraid. A cup of tea would be nice."

They went through to the café, resisted the tired-looking iced buns and sandwiches behind the plastic flaps and ordered a pot of tea for two. Bruce carried the tray with a stainless-steel pot and two white chipped mugs to a grey Formica table near the window away from the handful of other customers.

They sat for a moment gazing out of the window. Some teenage boys were playing five-a-side football watched by a small group of admiring girls, two of whom had babies in pushchairs. A younger boy had climbed almost to the top of the chain-link fence. Bruce could see that one of the sports centre staff was on the way round to tick him off.

Holly broke the silence. "Well, this is a bit surprising. I wasn't planning on sitting down to have tea with a copper when I came out this afternoon."

Bruce gave a half-smile and shrugged. "Wasn't my plan either to meet a...." He tailed off.

"A prostitute? Go on, say it. It's what I am. You won't catch anything just because you say the word."

Bruce shifted awkwardly in his seat and stirred his tea.

"Sorry." Holly smiled at him. "That was unfair. Look, neither of us really wants to talk about our work. I'll tell you what I want to know Bruce, and that is; what's a nice boy like you doing in a job like this?"

Bruce laughed. "Funny that, because I've been wanting to ask you the same question."

"I asked first. And in case you hadn't noticed I am not a boy. You tell me your story and I might tell you mine." There was a mischievous twinkle in her eyes. "No promises mind."

"Ok, why not. It's no big deal." Bruce took a swig of tea, swallowed hard and began to explain the various factors that had combined to bring him to this point in his life. He started with the family's move from London, the adjustment to a new school, his embarrassment about being a minister's son and inevitably his relationship with Jenny. Holly proved to be a good listener. She kept her eyes on his face as he spoke, nodded from time to time, smiled reassuringly and let Bruce speak without interruption. He was not used to this. His sisters and mother were all strong on expressing their views and weak on turn-taking. Even Jenny, in her vivacious way had seldom let Bruce talk at length without offering an observation or taking the conversation off at a tangent. He found himself speaking about his break-up with Jenny more fully and honestly than he had at any point since it had happened. Realizing that he was drawing near to the end of his account he wondered, whether he could say something about his issues at work. He decided that might be unwise. As he finished he looked out of the window. The soccer players and their gaggle of fans were drifting away. The pitch was empty.

"Thanks! That explains a lot." said Holly. "From that first time I met you behind the Chinese I knew you weren't a typical copper."

"People are joining from a much wider range of backgrounds now. Take Harpal for example. And there's a guy just arrived on one of the other shifts who studied at Cambridge." Bruce sensed he must sound as though he were protesting a little too much.

Holly nodded. "I know and that's a good thing I guess but," she hesitated, "Don't take this the wrong way Bruce. Do you ever think you might be wasting yourself, you know, selling yourself short?"

Bruce did not react. Holly could see that she had stung him. "Sorry!"

"It's ok," Bruce replied. "You sound like a cross between my old headmaster and my father. And yes, I know I might be under-achieving but right now this is where I am, so I must get on with it. No-one made my choices for me." He paused and looked at Holly. "I know we don't know each other well but seeing as you've raised the bar in the bluntness stakes, let me turn your question back on you. I'm not wondering if a smart looking, clever girl is selling herself short but frankly why is she selling herself at all?"

Bruce immediately regretted his directness. He had not meant to be unkind. Holly had seemed to crumple in the face of his question. She suddenly looked more fragile, diminished as she gazed down, studying the dregs in her mug.

"My turn to apologize. That was my clumsy way of saying you seem a good person and deserve more than this."

Holly continued to gaze into her mug, almost as though she were reading the tea-leaves, looking for inspiration. "How do you know what I deserve? You don't know me."

"Fair comment." said Bruce. He was relieved that she had broken her silence.

"I know you could report me, though I hope you've seen how discreet I try to be."

Called into Question

Bruce nodded.

"You've opened up to me, so I guess it's only fair I give you a bit in return. I understand what it means to have your heart broken. I really do."

Over the next twenty minutes Holly shared her story with Bruce. At first, she spoke falteringly, stopping to look out of the window from time to time ordering her thoughts. She spoke with little emotion and this surprised Bruce. It was as though she was recounting a sequence of events that had happened to someone else. Bruce wondered if that was her way of coping. He tried hard to listen to her as well as Holly had listened to him. His natural inquisitiveness meant that lots of questions sprang to mind as she spoke. He had to fight the urge to interrupt her.

Holly was, as her accent suggested, from an upper middle-class background. Her earliest memories were happy ones. She had lived with her mother and father in Virginia Water in Surrey. Her father had been a pilot; having qualified with the Air Transport Auxiliary towards the end of the Second World War he had gone on to have a successful career with BOAC. The family enjoyed a comfortable life-style. Holly attended a local private school before going away to a co-educational boarding school when she was thirteen. During her first year away from home her father had suddenly become ill with lung cancer. This had spread quickly to his liver and despite a radical course of chemo and radiotherapy he died within a year of the original diagnosis. As an only child Holly felt she had no-one close with whom to share her grief. She had withdrawn into herself. Being away at school meant that she felt detached from her mother's journey of grief.

Two years later, when she was just fifteen her mother announced to her during one exeat weekend that she had met a man and intended to marry him. Holly met this significant stranger during the following school holidays by which time he had moved in to the family home. She took an instant dislike to Angus. Although he appeared to have made her mother happy she was uneasy in his presence from the outset; with good reason as it turned out.

The family home was set in a large garden bordered by mature rhododendron and azalea bushes that provided brilliant swathes of colour and privacy from neighbours or passers-by. An elegant flight of stone steps led down from the terrace to a swimming pool complete with spring-board. The pool was screened by a trellis of rambling roses. Ever since she was a little girl Holly had treated the changing room, a pale blue cabin, as her own hide-away. It was her favourite place in the whole world. One afternoon during the long summer holidays, when her mother had gone to town, she had been swimming alone when Angus appeared from nowhere and dived in. Holly made her excuses and went to leave. To her horror he pulled down her bikini briefs as she climbed up the metal steps. She screamed but Angus was undeterred and treated it as a great joke. Over the following weeks he began to pester her at every opportunity, sometimes coming to her room at night. Holly could not understand why her mother could not see what was going on. Yet she also felt intensely guilty that she did not speak to her mother about it. As what had begun as inappropriate behaviour deteriorated into outright abuse Holly endured it in silence, passively acquiescing to Angus and his increasing demands.

She was relieved to return to school in the autumn. She threw herself in to her studies and in to a passionate relationship with a boy in the upper sixth. This was her first proper boyfriend. As Bruce listened to Holly relating these events he became conscious of some parallels in their two stories.

Within a month of her sixteenth birthday Holly had become pregnant. She was surprised to discover that the school was well practiced in dealing with such events. She was sent home, the official line being that she had contracted glandular fever. The school consulted her mother and between them they arranged for Holly to have an abortion in a London clinic near Regent's Park. Her boyfriend stayed on at school to complete his A-levels. His name was Tom and was now in London in the final year of his medical studies. Their relationship had not withstood the involvement of so many outraged adults.

Living back at home with her mother and Angus was a nightmare for Holly. In theory, she had been enrolled in a comprehensive school near her home. In practice she played truant increasingly, choosing to hang around with a group of art students in Guildford. She started to use drugs to dull her emotional pain though maintained she was never addicted to them. On her eighteenth birthday, she had started to receive a small allowance from a trust fund from her father's estate. When Angus began abusing her again she decided to leave. She wrote her mother a note detailing all that had happened, packed her things in two cases and travelled to Cheston one weekend while her mother and Angus were on a city-break to Paris.

"There you are. That's my tale of woe. Pretty disgusting really."

Bruce was taken aback by her matter-of-fact tone. He had sat listening with his elbow on the table and his right hand over his mouth to stop himself interrupting. As Holly finished and without thinking he reached across the table and gently touched her forearm. She immediately recoiled.

"Please don't. Don't be kind to me Bruce. I can't handle that."

"Holly, that's awful. But what I don't get, at all, is why, given all that, you are doing what you are doing?"

She looked at him. "Of course, you don't Bruce. You are a kind person, but your life has been easy. And you're a man."

Before he could respond, Holly got up to leave. "Thanks for the game and the tea. I expect I'll see you around." Bruce watched her leave, his mind racing.

Chapter 11

April 18th

£140 – bad week, missed two nights, curse!

Saw B at sports centre, there's more to him than I thought. Very fit. Gentle rather than wet, getting over a broken-heart, easy to talk to, good listener. I told him he was wasting himself in the police – he looked hurt even though he tried to hide it. Think I said too much. Am sure I did. First time for ages that I've told anyone all that stuff about home. Once I started it just kept coming. Thought he might be shocked but didn't seem to be. I was bit sharp with him – didn't mean to be. When I got back here I actually felt ok about it – not as angry as last time.

Nice parcel and letter from Auntie Sally, she sent some tights and couple of paperbacks – wonder what she thinks I'm doing. She'd have a fit. She wants to tell mum where I am, thinks it would be better but says she'll keep her promise if I want her to. I definitely do. Listening to myself spilling it all out to B it almost sounded like something that happened to somebody else. Wish it was. That's how I want it to be.

Chapter 12

Bruce took a deep breath and knocked on the door. Below the pane of frosted glass, a small typed card in a metal frame indicated that this was Detective Chief Inspector Collins's office. Alongside this innocuous name tag was a picture of former England and West Ham football captain Bobby Moore holding aloft the World Cup. Collins was proud of his roots in London's east-end. When Collins had learned, the previous year that his hero had been allowed to join second division outfit Fulham he had gone on a ten-hour drinking binge with his life-long friend Sgt. Phil Fleming. Bruce had heard that the two men had turned up for duty the following day as though nothing had happened.

"Yes! Come!" The man outlined through the glass was clearly in no mood for small talk in the exchange that was about to take place. As he opened the door Bruce found himself picturing Daniel being thrown into the lions' den. The story had excited him as a boy back in Sunday school days but now it had lost its' appeal. Bruce walked into the room and went to sit down on the chair in front of the large desk behind which DCI Collins was sat reading typed statements.

"Stay standing Hammond. This isn't going to take long, and I don't want your squeaky arse messing up my chair. Do you understand?"

"Yes, sir." Bruce stood, his hands clasped behind his back in the "at ease" parade ground stance. He could not have felt less at ease if he had tried.

"Do you know where I was last week Hammond?" Collins asked without looking up from the papers.

"On holiday, sir."

"Yes, on holiday. Golfing on the Spanish Algarve. And very nice it was too. Have you ever been to the Algarve Hammond?"

"No sir." Bruce knew he was not expected to make chit-chat. He braced himself for the moment that the conversation took a different turn as he knew it surely must.

"When I was your age and stage Hammond my typical holiday was a wet week in a B&B at Southend. Do you know why I enjoy relaxing in Spanish sunshine, with a villa and pool now?"
"No, sir."

"I'll give you three reasons. One: I've earned it. I know I've done a bloody good job as a copper to get where I am today, which is top of the pile. Two: I know I've got a damned good squad who all know how we do things, all singing off the same hymn-sheet - which of course is one thing I imagine you are an expert in Hammond, hymn sheets. And three: I am a long way away from smart-arse young know-it-alls like you."

Bruce looked at his feet.

"Look at me Hammond." Collins's voice was suddenly harsh and menacing. "I do not like having to come back to read reports like this from DC Finlay telling me that a rookie PC knows our business better than we do. This squad is judged by results like every other one in the country. We are the real business and I am not prepared to have the likes of you screwing up so much as one case."

Bruce shifted uneasily and went to speak.

"I don't want to hear a word from you, Hammond. I'm ending your CID placement here and now. If you can't follow instructions from officers who know how to do this job bloody well, then there is no place for you in my team. Not even for two more weeks."

"But sir..."

"Shut up, you piece of shite. You will re-join your shift tomorrow. You can explain yourself to Inspector Middleton."

"Sir."

Bruce went to turn away.

"You'll go when I say. One more thing I want to know. Are you queer

Hammond?"

"No, sir!" He was taken aback by this.

"Not chummy chummy with your dark friend? Pakkis and Dagos sticking close together. Very close together."

"No, sir." Bruce knew he was close to losing his temper. He recalled Harpal Shaik's advice about dealing with abuse from Collins. *"Don't give him the response he wants."*

"Oh no, of course you're not a poofter Brucie!" There was something more sinister creeping into his tone now. "You like the ladies don't you. One, in particular from, what I hear. Been sniffing round the tartlet on the High Street haven't you Hammond. The little miss who fancies herself. Too good for the truckers and honest working men. Only gets her kit off for the older men if they say please and thank you." Collins was studying Bruce's face carefully.

"That's shocked you hasn't it. I told you we do the job properly here. We don't miss a trick Hammond. You're well and truly screwed lad so don't you dare try and tell me or any of my men how to do our job. Personally, I think you better spend the next few days plodding the streets having second thoughts about being picky over what you can and can't say in court. Do we understand each other Hammond? I do hope so. 'Cos if we don't, the only hope you will ever have of seeing the Algarve is as a castrated pool-boy or barman. Got it?"

Bruce nodded and left. He felt sick.

Returning home early, he avoided his mother's curious inquiries. He had concocted a cover-story about a special operation in which they could only use bona fide CID officers.

"Don't worry darling. I am sure there will be plenty of other opportunities for you. I'll make you some toasted sandwiches? Cheese and pickle ok?"

Bruce felt that his mother was possibly the most positive person he had ever met. The family joked that if she had lived in an earlier era and been burned at the stake she would probably have said, "Oh my feet are lovely and warm!" Bruce often wondered if her sunny disposition was a conscious choice or the result of her Mediterranean heritage. Today their exchange reminded him of his school days. If, as had happened from time to time, he was kept back in detention as a punishment he had passed off his lateness as being due to a sports practice. His mother had never queried this or challenged him. Bruce suspected that she was not as gullible as she made out. He was grateful for her discretion. His father's Scottish Presbyterian background however meant that he had to tip-toe around him rather more carefully when it came to issues of honesty and morality.

He took his plate of toasties up to his room, lay on his bed, kicked off his shoes and flicked on the bedside radio. James Taylor's "How sweet it is to be loved by you" was playing. A sharp slap silenced that. Bruce lay looking at the ceiling lost in his thoughts until it was dark.

Next morning, he was back in uniform and into the station in good time for early shift. Word had clearly got around. None of his colleagues seemed surprised to see him. Bruce wondered if the almost over-friendly welcome was the result of someone having had a quiet word. There was a folded note sellotaped to his metal locker. *"Please come and see me at your lunch break. Insp. Middleton PS. NOT going to give you a bollocking."* Bruce crumpled up the note and put it in his tunic pocket. The Inspector's reassuring PS was characteristically kind.

"Come in Bruce, make yourself comfortable." Bob Middleton was one of those men who always made eye contact when talking to you. Bruce guessed he must be in his late thirties. His smile was warm and disarming. The contrast with the meeting the previous day was stark. "Ok, so I've read DCI Collins's notes, but I'd like to hear your version of events. No hurry. I've asked Gareth to cover your beat for the next hour."

Bruce began to recount the events surrounding the arrest of the black youngster for possession of drugs. He felt his recall was good, not least because he had gone back over things repeatedly since that day on patrol with DC Finlay. Inspector Middleton stopped him from time to time to clarify a detail.
When Bruce ended his account, the older man looked at him kindly. "Anything else you want to say?"

Bruce hesitated. Ever since he had read the note at the beginning of the shift he had wondered if this was the opportunity to talk about the beating he had witnessed in his first weeks at Cheston. "No point holding back now" he thought. Over the next five minutes he outlined what had happened to the unfortunate Peter Larkin. Even without recounting the details aloud images from that cell sickened him. His superior listened without comment. When Bruce appeared to have finished the Middleton allowed him space for his thoughts before asking a leading question.

"Why do you feel so strongly Bruce, about this sort of thing?"

Bruce looked across the desk, checking that this was not a trick question. He detected no cunning or malice in Bob Middleton's face.

"You really want to know sir?" Middleton nodded.

"I guess for all sorts of reasons. For starters what is the point of spending so much time in our training having the importance drummed into us of following Judges' Rules and procedures carefully if, out on the street, we drive a coach and horses through the whole thing? Seriously, we must have spent hours on that stuff. Since being here I've been told it's just like how you drive before your driving test, once you've passed it doesn't matter. That can't be right, can it sir?"

Middleton was listening carefully. "Go on, I want to hear why you personally think it is so important. It's not simply because you resent having wasted time at Eynsham, is it?"

Called into Question

"No, it isn't. I know I've got lots to learn, I really do but surely if we are meant to be upholding and enforcing the law we must do that right. If we become a law unto ourselves, if we beat people up, tidy up evidence to get a result, as I see it, that must mean we're undermining the law – not strengthening it. I think it calls into question the whole basis of what we do. It's like this, sir; do you remember the foot and mouth outbreak a few years ago?"

"I certainly do. 1967. My father-in-law had a farm in Shropshire. He lost his whole herd and that finished him off as far as farming was concerned. He runs a newsagents in Shrewsbury now. Sorry, what's your point Bruce?"

"Well, all those animals were destroyed to stop the disease and to prevent it getting into the food-chain. I don't understand why people can't see that every time we cut a corner or lie in court it's like we're infecting the legal system in the same way." Bruce was on a roll now.

"And if that's big picture stuff then there's another reason. I don't like seeing people being treated unfairly. That pathetic kid wasn't the full deal up top mentally. I mean we nicked him and he got a beating as well. I can't see how that is serving society. He needed help, not punishment."

The Inspector sighed. "The report that came down with you from your training was right. You are indeed a thinker, aren't you? Now don't take this the wrong way, but that is not going to make life easy for you. I know you've discovered that already."

"Harpal Shaik says I have to learn to be more patient sir."

"Well he's right Bruce, but off the record I would encourage you not to lose sight of that principle of keeping the legal food chain uncontaminated. I like that. I really do. If you can get through these early years you could go a long way in the Force, a very long way, but you are going to have to pick your battles carefully. You are right, these things will come back to haunt us."

"Sir, if you don't mind me asking? Why don't people like you and Gareth speak up? Gareth told me he's had to turn a blind eye to stuff over the years."

"I can't speak for him, but I know that I am doing the best I can in my own way. We all must look at ourselves in the mirror each morning and ask if we are being true to ourselves and what we believe and value. I am not going to tell you how I do that."
"Sorry sir, I didn't mean to be rude?" Bruce said, regretting his question.

"I know you didn't Hammond, but you do have an unfortunate habit of appearing rude and rather full of yourself at times."

Bruce noted the formality that had crept into Inspector Middleton's tone.

"As I was saying, I do what I can when I can and try and keep my eye on my longer term aims. I advise you to do the same. So, this is why I have agreed with DCI Collins a way forward that I hope will get us all out of this little mess."

Bruce had not expected the conversation to take such a turn.

"The lad who was arrested is pleading guilty to a lesser charge which means his case won't have to go to Crown Court. What you didn't know is that he has a previous conviction for drug possession? DC Finlay didn't tell you that. I am sending you on a two-week residential driving course which will coincide with the hearing at the magistrates. Your statement will reflect your pocket book entry. You were smart omitting the line about seeing him carrying the sports bag. The good news is you won't be required to perjure yourself in court. With any luck, you probably won't even have to appear. Satisfied?"

Bruce was speechless, completely taken by surprise.

"Thank you, sir. That's brilliant. Just one thing though I don't get. Why isn't that lad defending himself? On the day, he was outraged. I was sure him or his lawyer would lodge a complaint."

Bob Middleton shuffled the papers on his desk. "Ah well, two reasons there. As I said, the lad had a previous conviction which means the drugs either were his, or he's taking a hit for his mates. I also understand from the powers on high, the DCI and his friends, that the lad's mother runs a knocking-shop, two doors along from the Afro-Caribbean Club and was about to be busted. Strangely that case is going to be dropped for lack of evidence. Do you get my drift?"

Called into Question

Bruce nodded though he was still digesting the consequences of these revelations.

"Just two more things PC Hammond before I let you go. If anyone asks if you'd like to go down to the Afro-Caribbean for a Red Stripe, my advice is to make an excuse and move on smartly. Also, be a little more careful over how and with whom you spend your time off. A nod's as good as a wink to a blind horse. Ok."

Bruce nodded, thanked the Inspector and left.

Chapter 13

April 25th

£120 – evenings warmer but lighter, win some you lose some. TC very rough and threatening, have bought spot cover-up for marks. Met A-M, Belgian girl who works the lorry park for a coffee yesterday morning. Things not good down there. So glad I never got involved. She says one of the Rumanian girls has disappeared. A-M has bought a flick-knife. She showed me it – elegant and innocent looking but very sharp. Am wondering whether to get one myself. She said she could get it one for me. There's a range of colours – bit bizarre.

Think B is in trouble. In fact, I know he is – kicked off CID placement. HS seems to be keeping his head down. Auntie Sal would love him - looks like Omar Sharif. Nothing from her for a bit. Hope she's ok.

Rent's going up next month – bloody rogue.

Chapter 14

After a couple of days back on the beat Bruce realized he no longer felt hurt or embarrassed by the premature ending of his CID placement. The routine of the High Street had a soothing effect. Seeing the delivery drivers, acknowledging familiar faces of cabbies, street cleaners, and bus drivers helped him to regain his equilibrium. Even the gentle banter with the winos who shuffled to and fro between the churchyard and the bus station was reassuring.

Bruce told Harpal the full story about the CID debacle over a couple of frames of snooker one lunchtime. He thanked his friend for the advice about not rising to Collins's bait.

"There's one thing I don't understand, and it bothers me."

"What's that?" Harpal was lining up a tricky shot along the side cushion into the far pocket.

"I don't know how Collins knew about Holly. I've gone over and over it but not come up with anything."

"Bruce, one of the things I learned on my placement is that CID have a comprehensive network of informers throughout the town at every level. You could say it's the mark of good policing. Believe me they have eyes and ears everywhere."

"I suppose so, but it felt quite sinister being on the receiving end of it."

"How is the lady of the night by the way?" asked Harpal missing an easy red to the middle as he spoke.

"Holly? I don't know. Obviously, I've not seen her over this last week. I haven't got a total career death wish. Well, not yet I haven't."

*   *   *   *

"Control calling all units. Need presence at 149 Tanners Lane. Report of distressed man in flats. Out."

"Kilo 17 to control I can be there in five, over."

"Control to Kilo 17. Ok make your way there ASAP. Control out."

As Bruce set off he heard Harpal Shaik's distinctive voice. "Kilo 14 to Control. Am also near – shall I attend. Kilo 14 out."

"Thanks Kilo 14 might be a good idea. Control out."

149 Tanners Lane was a shabby looking Edwardian building divided into flats. In its' heyday it had been a respectable villa with views from the rear towards Windsor Castle. Bruce and Harpal Shaik arrived almost simultaneously from opposite directions. They were met by three worried looking residents standing together on the steps that led to a communal front door. A young

Called into Question

woman in her twenties, dressed in cheap pyjamas and holding a toddler tightly in her arms called out, "Quick, he's going to set fire to the whole place."

Harpal took control. "Okay calm down. It's going to be ok."

"It won't be ok if he sets light to himself, like what he's threatening to do." A middle-aged man in a string vest and grey flannels chipped in.

"That's right; he's completely flipped, really bad this time." This was the offering from the third member of the welcoming committee; a woman with peroxide blonde hair in her fifties. She had a cigarette on the go.

"Bruce, get on to Control. We need Fire Brigade and an ambulance just in case.
Quick as they can just to be on the safe side." While Bruce called for support, Harpal turned back to the residents. "Ok. Someone give me the basics – who are we talking about here? Which flat? Please put that cigarette out."

The younger woman took the initiative. "I'm the one who called you. It's Leon in Flat 2 on the first floor. He's a Rasta and his head is all over the place. He's been in the mental unit up the hospital for a few weeks, but he came home last week. He's not right. He started shouting first thing this morning and we could hear him throwing things around in his flat. He's done that before but it's worse today. He threw his radio out of the window into the backyard. Cynth and I went and knocked on his door."

The older woman took up the story. "Normally when he's having one of his turns he'll open the door to us, but he just kept shouting 'Go away. I've got to burn it down – it's the only way'. He's got a can of petrol he uses for his moped."

Harpal put his hand on her arm to stop her going on. "Thanks. Anyone else in the building apart from him?"

This time the man responded. "Yes, Brenda's in her flat on the same floor. She's bed-ridden, never comes out. And she's deaf so we can't get through to her."

Suddenly, there was a loud bang and the sound of breaking glass.

"Back-up on its way Harpal but I think we should go in now."

"Yeah. Ok. Right, listen carefully please. I want all of you to go down onto the pavement and wait there. Thank you. I'm sure it'll be ok."

The two men went into the building. The communal hallway stank of cats but masking this was the unmistakable sickly-sweet smell of petrol. "Don't touch the lights, Bruce! This place could go up in flames."

The first-floor landing was dark. Even in the gloom they could see from gouges in the door frame of Flat 2 that the current occupant or a previous tenant had tried to force the lock on more than one occasion. Bruce and Harpal stood listening a moment. From inside they could hear the scrape of furniture being moved and the splashing of liquid.

"Leon, Leon!" Harpal knocked gently on the door. "It's going to be ok Leon. Can you open the door for us? We want to help you."

"Go away. I don't need help. Jah's helping me. He's told me what to do. He wants a burnt offering- it's the only way." His voice was deep, but Leon sounded breathless in his confusion.

"Leon, my name's Bruce. Please let us in. Jah loves you. He doesn't want you to hurt yourself."

"No, man. I've heard him. Fire's the only way. Water can't do it. I've tried bleach. It's got to be the flames."

Bruce could hear sirens getting nearer. Suddenly from inside the flat there was a loud metallic crash as Leon hurled a petrol can against the door. Bruce and Harpal recoiled instinctively. Without thinking Bruce, leading with his right shoulder threw himself against the door. It gave way under his force, the frame splintering as he lurched into the squalid room. Instantly, his senses heightened by his adrenaline rush, he took stock of what confronted him. Newspapers, girlie mags and boxes of tablets were strewn across the carpet-less floor. Leon was startled, wild-eyed, sitting on the side of his bed in a black vest and his underpants. Petrol was dripping from his dreadlocks, was on his face and had soaked his clothes. He had a Swan Vesta matchbox in his right hand and was holding three of the red-tipped matches between the thumb and first two fingers of his left. He was on the point of striking them.

Using the momentum of his forced entry Bruce launched himself in a dive towards the troubled man. He hit him chest on and knocked the box out of his hand. He heard Leon's ribs crack and knew he had winded him.

Harpal was close behind, trying to bring calm into the chaos. "Great job mate. Just keep him there. Ok Leon, it's over. You're going to be all right. We're going to make sure you're safe now."

Bruce could feel Leon struggling to breathe under his weight. All the fight had gone from him. He shifted his bulk slightly to give him a chance to draw breath. At that point, they were aware of voices on the stairway.

"In here." Harpal called.

Two firemen and a paramedic appeared in the doorway, followed by a young woman in a brown coat carrying a black case.

"I'm Doctor Newell, Leon's GP. I'll sedate him, then we'll get him back to the psychiatric unit at Wexham Park. I told them he wasn't ready."

Bruce stood up gingerly. His shoulder was hurting. He felt numb.
One of the firemen took control of the situation. "Ok. Doc do your stuff. And then we'll get everyone out. This place isn't going to be safe for a bit. I gather there's an old lady next door. We'll sort her out too."

Bruce and Harpal made their way downstairs. Stepping out in to the daylight they took huge gulps of fresh air to clear the smells and sights that had assaulted their senses. Bruce realized he stank of petrol and pungent body odour. Word had travelled fast. A dozen or so neighbours had joined the residents on the pavement. They broke into spontaneous applause as Bruce and Harpal appeared.

A police car turned into the road. Inspector Middleton got out. "Well, Butch Cassidy and the Sundance Kid strike again. Well done you two. Get in. We'll get you cleaned up. Paper work can wait."

At the end of the shift Harpal asked Bruce if he fancied going over to the canteen for a drink and a bite to eat. "No thanks mate. I'd better head home. I still reek of petrol and stuff. A good soak in the bath is what I need and some home comforts. See you tomorrow."

Bruce arrived back at The Manse just as his family was finishing their evening meal. His parents had always placed great store on the importance of sitting down to eat together at least once in the day.

"Oh darling, what a nice surprise!" said his mother when Bruce put his head round the door. "I wish you'd said you would be back early. We could have waited for you."
"Pooh. You stink!" said his younger sister, holding her nose.

"Thank you, I know I do! I just need a bath and some space to think."

His father looked at him carefully. "You ok son? Tough day?"

Bruce hesitated; he knew he was not in the mood for a discussion about his day and the lessons that could be learned about humanity from it. He knew his father's concern for him was genuine and well-intended and yet inside he felt like a powder keg ready to explode at any moment.

"Depends what you mean by tough? Alongside the duplicating machine jamming or losing the flower rota, no it was a piece of cake! Just some poor sod at the end of his tether setting fire to himself. You know the normal run of the day stuff."

"He said "sod" Mum!" His sister was picking up neither his sarcasm nor his distress.

"No need to be sarcastic, Bruce. Your father is only trying to be sympathetic. We do know about the tougher side of life, don't forget."

"Do you? Do you really? Listen while you and Dad are planning the next Bring & Buy Sale or Sunday School outing, there are people out in the real world struggling to make sense of all the crap that comes their way!"

"Bruce that will do. I won't have you speak to your mother like that. I suggest you go and have a bath. We can talk later when you've calmed down."

"No, we won't talk later Dad. You know what you can do. You can take your bloody faith and shove it. It doesn't work out there in the real world. It just doesn't work." With this parting shot Bruce slammed the door and went upstairs to his room. His mind was racing. He was cross with himself for having lost his temper. He dumped his stinking uniform in the corner of the room and retreated to the bathroom, taking a bottle of rum with him.

Bruce lay in the bath trying to order his thoughts and control his emotions. He knew he had been unfair on his parents but was less clear about what he really felt. Lying back with his head almost fully submerged he could hear noises from the water and heating system like distant underworld echoes. The bathroom ceiling was Artex with random swirls and ridges around a half globe light fitting – the work of a plasterer in his experimental period. He let his eyes follow one extravagant line of plaster attempting block out his jumbled thoughts. He was unsuccessful on both counts.

Why was he so angry? The obvious conclusion was that it was a delayed reaction to the incident with Leon. But what had he felt? Bruce didn't recall feeling scared. At the time, he had done what needed to be done. There had scarcely been time for thought. He remembered being surprised by the applause of the neighbours when they emerged from the building. Probably as much an expression of relief on their part as it was expression of gratitude. Going over the sequence of events, viewing them like film clips, he was more aware of what a brush with danger the whole episode had been.

Bruce reached for his rum and ran some more hot water. He lay back again and watched water running into the overflow outlet. This had a been a boyhood pleasure when he was growing up. Deliberate naughtiness, persisting until one of his parents noticed water splashing in the side alley of their old house and called out to him.

His thoughts turned to the tragic Leon, living in squalid confusion, his disordered mind fixated on some version of God that Bruce did not recognize. He recalled his own words to the troubled young man. He had tried to reassure him of divine love but had failed to get through to him. Bruce had spoken instinctively, as the situation demanded. Now on reflection he wondered whether that was merely from expediency or from some deeper vestige of his childish faith.

"Bruce, the water's overflowing." His mother's muffled voice from downstairs.

"Yes, big deal." he muttered.

Chapter 15

Inspector Middleton was as good as his word. Within a fortnight Bruce found himself at the force driving school in Aylesbury on a residential driving course. He had passed his civilian driving test within months of his seventeenth birthday. His parents had been glad of his help as an extra taxi driver ferrying his sisters to and from ballet and music lessons. In return, he had been able to use the family car to take Jenny on dates further afield. The battered Vauxhall estate was unreliable; Bruce had learned from bitter experience the importance of parking on a slope to make bump starting easier. In time, his grandfather helped him to buy his own car, the Mini, but because of the early experiences he was still under-confident when it came to overtaking.

"For God's sake Hammond, when I say go you go. If you miss another overtake I shall take the wheel and put you over the other side of the road myself." Bruce knew the instructor was not joking. The course members were teamed up three to a car. He had seen the instructor take the unorthodox step of hitting a colleague's hand with the short cane he carried and gripping the top of the wheel to put the unmarked Ford Granada on the other side of the road. Sitting in the back was more nerve-wracking than driving.

The two-week course was highly intensive. Initially it was like being a learner all over again as Bruce and the others adjusted to a new driving system. Breaking old habits was difficult. He learned how to read the vanishing points on bends so that he could set the car up to take them at the maximum speed.

The fact that they were using unmarked cars meant that unsuspecting motorists did not take kindly to being cut up as Bruce and his colleagues miscalculated high speed manoeuvres. Only when the bright coloured car had flashed by did other motorists realize the four passengers were uniformed police officers. As the course progressed so the excursions took them further afield. Each of the three drove a long stretch, giving commentary as they went. Late in the course there was an afternoon on a skid pan which proved to be the most enjoyable session of the fortnight.

The last Friday was test day. During breakfast, Bruce overhead the four instructors discussing where they fancied going that day. Given that it was a bright late spring day the consensus was that a trip to the Wye Valley would fit the bill. Bruce found himself being assessed driving at speed through the Forest of Dean heading for Tintern Abbey. There was little traffic on the road as they drove through the heavily-wooded, steep-sided valley. He wondered how many times he could get away with mentioning the danger of loose sheep in his commentary. Bizarrely, the opening lines from Wordsworth's poem about Tintern suddenly came to mind, like a distracting ear-worm, a relic of his "O" level English Literature course. *"Five years have past; five summers, with the length of five long winters."* He resisted an irrational urge to recite the poem aloud.

Arriving back in Aylesbury, Bruce was relieved to discover that he was now authorized to drive police vehicles. The prospect of becoming a panda driver opened before him.

Called into Question

Driving home that evening, putting his Mini through its' paces on twisting lanes through Chiltern beech woods he realized that he had been totally absorbed in the course and had hardly given the difficult court case a second thought. As he drove past an old half-timbered pub near Penn he also recognized that Jenny was intruding on his thoughts less frequently.

The driving course had also been timely for domestic life at The Manse. Like a summer storm that will not break there had been an unspoken tension since his mealtime outburst. His parents had not attempted to broach the subject and Bruce had not felt inclined to apologize. For the moment sleeping dogs were being left to lie. Over supper Bruce regaled the family with tales about his motoring exploits from the previous fortnight.

"What was the fastest you drove?" asked Hannah.

"One day on the motorway I did over a hundred. It was really exciting."

"You will be careful won't you darling?"

"Yes mother, I will. And I will try not to talk to any strange men either!"

"Don't be like that. It's only because I love you."

"I know you do Mum, but in case you haven't noticed, I am a man now."

"Once a parent, always a parent." His father had a seemingly endless store of pithy aphorisms – a legacy of nearly thirty years of preaching to the faithful.

"You'll never guess who I bumped into in Caley's in Windsor today?" His mother enjoyed a weekly shopping expedition in the royal town.

"You're right, I won't."

His mother continued undeterred. "Rose, Jenny's mother. She was just coming out of lingerie."

Bruce felt his stomach turn. He tried to look calm.

"What did she have to say?" asked his father.
"Jenny's doing very well, still enjoying the course. She's become friendly with a junior doctor from Surrey. He's called Tom I think."

Bruce felt that his parents were at times remarkably insensitive for people who prided themselves on their pastoral concern. He pushed his plate away and got up from the table.
"Well thank you for that news update. Very kind." He slammed the door on his way out.

Bruce flicked through his LPs in the rack by his bed. He picked out his most recent Barclay James Harvest album, *Everyone is Everybody Else*. Placing it on the turntable, he turned up the volume and sank down on to his bed. He put his hands behind his head and lay looking at the ceiling. His thoughts were racing, any sense of calm eluding him. He knew he was being unfair on his family, especially on his parents. Perhaps he should apply for a room in the single men's quarters after all. Despite the frustrations of home life and his parents' apparent inability to see him as a working man he knew that shutting himself into a small bedroom on police premises every night might not be the best thing for him in his present state of mind.

Why had his mother felt the need to tell him about meeting Jenny's mum? He did not want to know what she was up to. Yet as soon as he thought this he realized it was not the case. What had she said? Jenny was friendly with a junior doctor from Surrey. He recognized the euphemism for what it was. There was something more. Bruce concentrated, mulling over his mother's words. His favourite track on the album was playing, Paper Wings

Oh, can you see him now?
A broken man without a dream
Oh, can you hear him now?
A futile laugh above the screams

Was that him? It couldn't be. Nineteen and without dreams, surely not. Other words echoed in his head. He had been unable to set aside Holly's challenge to him, her observation that he was selling himself short. He struggled to convince himself that it wasn't the case. He reflected too on his outburst at his parents. "*You can shove your faith – it doesn't work out there in the real world.*" He remembered the shock hearing the words coming from his mouth as he said them. It was like being disembodied, a spectator on the scene. With the emotional checks and brakes off was that what he really felt? He had not flung it out as a cheap shot to wound his parents, but he knew they were deeply hurt.

Bruce had explored intellectual objections to faith with friends in the sixth form. Issues around how a God of love could allow suffering had been aired in general studies sessions and occasionally over drinks in a pub. Bruce remembered that at the time questions of ethics and morality had bothered him more, as he and Jenny had become more intimate. Was that what religion is about? A control mechanism in the hands of the older generation, designed to put young people on a guilt trip?

"A junior doctor called Tom!" That was it – the phrase that had bugged him. Oh God! No, that couldn't be. He remembered Holly telling him that her ex-boyfriend was called Tom and had studied medicine. He was from Surrey. Surely not, that would just be too random, too bizarre.

*   *   *   *

"Come in. Let me introduce you. This is my father and mother. Papa, Ma this is Bruce." Harpal's parents stood in their hallway, smiled and bowed slightly to Bruce.

"Nameste. Welcome to our home. Our son's friend is our friend."
Harpal had advised Bruce not to expect a handshake but to return the greeting in kind. Bruce bowed with his palms together in front of him as though praying.

"It is very nice to meet you. Thank you for inviting me."

"This is one of my brothers, Radhesh, he'll prefer you to call him Raddy." Raddy offered his hand and Bruce shook it. Raddy was in jeans and a sweatshirt like Harpal.

"My eldest brother, Daman is married and with his family today."
At this point two teenage girls in traditional costume, but wearing aprons appeared from the kitchen. "And these are my sisters. Jaba and Madhu. The girls smiled. Bruce raised his right hand in greeting and giggling they returned to the kitchen.

Bruce was shown in to the front room and offered a mango juice with ice in a tall glass. It tasted different from any juice he had ever tried, sweet and exotic. Harpal, his father and brother sat and chatted while the women finished preparing the meal. They were interested in Bruce's family background. He asked them about their life in Nairobi and how they had dealt with the upheaval and adjustment they had been through. Bruce thought he detected a tear or two as Harpal's father described their former life with fondness and a dignified sadness. Bruce could see where his friend got his characteristic calmness.

The men were called through to a large dining room at the back of the house. When they were all seated the sisters brought round bowls and towels so that they could wash their hands.

"You sit here, Bruce. You are welcome to dig in with the rest of us, but my mother has given you a spoon, so don't feel you are on show!" The rest of the family laughed at this. Soon they were all dipping pieces of naan breads into the array of dishes on the table. Bruce noticed that the action of dipping the bread or taking portions using the right hand was very deliberate, only the tips of the fingers touched the food.

Bruce recognized stuffed tomatoes and tucked into a potato dish called aloo badiyan rasedaar which he assumed was a type of vegetable curry. At home, his family rarely tried foreign food. Bruce felt as though a window was opening on a parallel world.

"Would you like to try some kheer for dessert, Bruce?" asked Harpal's mother. She had kept her fine features and had a soft voice.

Harpal laughed and before Bruce could reply said, "It's not really an option!"

"What is it?"

"It is milk, rice and dried fruits, very simple, very easy on the stomach." said his mother spooning a generous helping into a silver bowl. Bruce was just about to take a first mouthful when Harpal's father asked him a question he had not anticipated.

"Has Harpal told you about his fiancée, Padmakshi?"

Bruce hoped the look of shock on his face was only momentary. He bought himself a second or two by taking a sip of water from the tumbler in front of him. Harpal shot him a meaningful glance across the table.

"He doesn't say a lot about her. But then he is quite private at work. We both are – it's safer that way."

"Ah yes. The outsiders, Butch somebody or other and the Sundance Kid aren't you."

Bruce was glad his answer seemed to have distracted the older man.
"She is very beautiful. Her name means lotus-eyed and suits her. They are going to marry next year when she has finished her accountancy exams. She is from a very good family. They are as happy as we are about the arrangement." Harpal's mother was clearly a big fan.

For his part Harpal said nothing, he kept his head down and concentrated on his kheer.

"We are looking forward to her taking on the books and tax for the shop." It appeared that business considerations had played no small part in the choice of bride.

"I don't mean this rudely in any way, but it sounds very um, very…odd to hear about parents choosing a bride for a son. I know my mother would love to do that, but I could only marry someone I had fallen in love with."

Harpal coughed quietly and Bruce hoped he had not overstepped the mark. He also noticed that Raddy was suddenly fascinated by his own dessert. The sisters laughed, and this lightened the atmosphere. Their father looked at Bruce kindly.

"It must seem strange to you I know. In your culture, you fall in love and then marry. In ours we marry and then fall in love. Parents try to choose wisely for the children they love. Harpal tells me your father is a priest. No doubt, he must pray about his children and their destinies."

Bruce considered this. He had not thought about this subject before. He would not want his parents involved in his choice and yet there was something about the explanation that appealed to him. He thought better of pursuing the discussion. He was looking forward to quizzing Harpal about the marriage plans. He was surprised his friend had not so much as hinted that his marital future was being mapped out. He felt a fleeting sense of disappointment.

"Do you have a girlfriend Bruce?"

"No, Mrs. Shaik I don't, not at the moment."

"I'm surprised."

"Ma, can we change the subject. Bruce does not need your help finding *him* a wife, that's for sure." Harpal grinned at Bruce and mouthed "thank you" as they got up from the table and went back into the sitting room to finish the meal with tea poured from an ornate pot.

Called into Question

Chapter 16

£65 – can't have too many weeks like that. Took a hit off Indian business man, cos I wouldn't give him a bj. Won't go with him again. Told TC.
Bloody rash has come back.
Haven't seen Bruce around – clearly in trouble. He won't last. Shame.
Have decided to get a knife. Meeting A-M next week. Haven't chosen a colour.
Pleased with new sketches - castle outline from the bridge.

Chapter 17

Bruce did not have to wait long before he had the chance to quiz his friend about the revelations over the Shaik dinner table. During the following week, they were both detailed for prisoner escort. This involved being locked in the back of a police van with three or four remand prisoners who were being taken from Cheston Magistrates court to Wandsworth Prison in South London.

The first time Bruce had done the "Paddy Wagon run", he had found it profoundly depressing. He had sat opposite a handcuffed teenager who had been over-partial to other people's smart cars. The lad was being held on remand before sentencing a few weeks later. This was going to be his first time in prison and the fear showed in his eyes on the rare occasions he lifted his head and looked at Bruce. One of the other prisoners, a seasoned con in his thirties, had made it worse with his black humour. "Wandsworth's the pits, a hard old place. They still test the frigging gallows a couple of times a year. What's the bloody point in that? Bastards!"

The journey to Wandsworth was usually painfully slow. The tortuous progress round the South Circular Road allowed plenty of time for quiet reflection. On that first prison trip, Bruce had found himself wondering at what point the young car thief's life had taken a wrong turn.
On this occasion, their consignment of flawed humanity duly delivered, Bruce and Harpal chatted as they bounced around in the back of the van heading west out of London.

"Thanks for covering for me over dinner at my place; I know that was awkward for you. I'm sorry my mum quizzed you. Hope it didn't upset you."

"That's ok. No, it was fine. I don't get so upset now. Not that I'm over Jenny yet but I'm getting there. I really enjoyed meeting your family. And that food was fab. I felt well and truly honoured."

"You were. They have never entertained a white person at home since they came to England. You're the first."

"Seriously?"

"Yeah, seriously. Back in Nairobi I remember that lots of Pa's business associates used to come to our house. From all sorts of racial groups – and believe me that wasn't typical. I think they have felt ashamed about our small house. Part of the shock of being displaced." Harpal looked wistful as he spoke.

"Well I really enjoyed it. Do thank them."

"I suppose you want to know about Padmakshi?"

"Well, I was a little intrigued, shall we say? Engagement is not exactly a small matter, is it? I was a bit surprised that you'd never mentioned it before." Bruce hoped the sense of disappointment he had felt over his friend's secrecy did not show too much.

"I'm sorry Bruce. I really am. I nearly told you about it last month when you told me about Jenny. I kicked myself after for having bottled it." Bruce could see that Harpal was genuinely embarrassed.

"The thing is that I suppose I live my life in two compartments. I've had to ever since we first arrived here in England. It was the only way to survive. When I told my parents that I was going to apply to go in the police they were shocked. They simply could not believe it. They felt I was rejecting my culture and their plans for me to go into the business. In all the discussions and arguments, I had to buy myself some time and space. I tried to reassure them that I was still proud of my heritage and obedient to them. Out of the blue they asked me if I was going to marry a white girl. I promised them I wouldn't."

At that moment, the van had to brake sharply as they joined the M4 at the Chiswick flyover. Bruce and Harpal were thrown against the metal partition. Harpal was interrupted in full flow.

"Wow, given your liking for shapely white girls that was quite a promise!"

"Thanks for stating the obvious Bruce. Yes, I regretted it as soon as I had said it. Anyway, having given ground over the police as they saw it, my parents went into over-drive with the engagement. To be honest I have let them get on with it. They are pretty much an unstoppable force."

"Harpal, are you telling me you are going to let your parents choose the woman you will spend the rest of your life with, who you will have children with?"

"Padmakshi really is beautiful. She's clever and has a nice personality and..."

Bruce cut off his friend in mid-sentence. "I know all that. Your mother told me! I can't imagine what it feels like to let your parents run your life like that. Different when we are kids, but Harpal, you and I are men now! There's no way I'd let my parents dictate to me like that."

"I dare say you wouldn't, but you are still more influenced by your parents than you like to think. At least in my culture the role of the parents is defined and what they do is done openly. English families pressurize their young people just as much to conform – they just do it more subtly." Harpal was fully into his stride, as though he were controlling a rally on the squash court.

"I tell you what, my friend. If you were to announce to your family that you were dating one of my sisters, you'd be amazed at the arguments your folks would pull out to convince you it was not a good idea. Or better still, imagine their faces if they discovered you were falling for a prostitute!"

"Whoa – hold on. You don't know my parents; your sisters are too young, and I don't fancy Holly."

"I may not know your parents Bruce, but I know your culture better than you know mine. I have to, so I can survive in it."

Bruce sensed he had been out-maneuvered.

"Anyway, I don't fancy Holly."

"You said!"

"Yes, but I don't!"

"Why are you going on about her then?"

"I'm not!"

"Listen to yourself Bruce. Listen carefully; you've got a lot going on in your head. I don't know how you live with the noise in there. As for me, in time I will probably marry Padmakshi and we'll make a good marriage and raise a strong family. I know my destiny."

The van braked hard again at the bottom of the slip-road as they turned off for Cheston.

"When the time comes I hope you'll do me the honour of coming to join in the celebrations. My sisters will be thrilled." With this Harpal grinned and winked, signaling the conversation was over.

A week later the shift was back on night duty. Bruce was the cover panda car driver which meant he took on any of the six panda beats if someone else was off ill or on holiday. Over the summer months, he was often in a car rather than on foot. In the middle of the week he was covering the town centre. As the night quietened down he decided to call in on his favourite Chinese take-away and help them deal with any of the evening's leftovers. He parked behind the parade of shops and walked to the back door.

"Well hello stranger! Have you been avoiding me?" Holly was sat on the bin they had shared the first time they had met, balancing a portion of chips on her lap. She had spread a paper napkin over her knees to protect her red leather mini-skirt from the fat.

"Oh hi! I wasn't expecting to bump into you. And erm, no I've not been avoiding you. We haven't seen you down the sports centre for a while."

"I've been busy."

"Good for you, rushed off your feet?" Bruce seemed incapable of opening a conversation with Holly without embarrassing himself.

"You really have a way with words don't you PC Hammond!"

"Sorry Holly! I wasn't trying to be funny."

"I know you weren't. It's ok. Tables are turned from the first time we met. Would you like to share my chips – if I eat all these I'll struggle getting in and out of this skirt? I won't bite, and no-one can see us. Come and squeeze alongside me."

Bruce reflected that Holly was well-practiced in putting men at ease. He perched on the large bin alongside her. He recognized her perfume as *Smitty*; light with a hint of fruitiness.

"How's your war with the baddies going? Winning?"
Bruce blew on a chip to cool it down. "Hardly. I'm beginning to think it's not a winnable battle. The whole culture of the force seems entrenched. Even the decent guys quietly accept stuff. They keep their heads down and get on with it."

"Do you think you'll stick at it?"

"I know you think I'm wasting my time but to be honest I'm not sure what else I want to do."

"Poor Brucie, you're a bit lost aren't you." Holly leaned against him as she said this. Feeling her shoulder against his upper arm stirred him unexpectedly. He shifted his weight away from her slightly.

"You're really rather shy, aren't you?" she said patting his thigh.

"No, I'm not!" he protested, "but *you* are a tease!"
"Tricks of the trade darling! That's all."

"Have you been drinking Holly? You've never flirted with me before."

"Sorry Bruce. No, I've not been drinking. Just forcing myself to be cheerful."

"Why tonight especially?" Bruce looked across at her, trying to make eye contact.
Holly was staring at a spot on the ground miles below her. She shook her head slightly.
"Has something happened?" Bruce regretted his directness.

"Bruce there is always something happening in my work, in my life. Normally I make sure I stay in control, keep to my own boundaries. But earlier tonight, no you don't want to hear this!" She shook her head again and tried to suppress a sob.

Without thinking Bruce put his arm round her. She stiffened momentarily and then leaned against him, sobbing uncontrollably. Bruce held her. He stayed quiet until she regained her composure.

"Want to tell me about it?"

"No, not really." Holly sat quietly for a few moments, her heels drumming lightly against the bin as she swung her legs back and forward. Sarah, Bruce's sister did that when she was either anxious or excited.

"You know, despite your work you don't have to put up with anything. The law still protects you."

"The law protects me! Bruce, don't be naïve. The law doesn't protect me."

Holly jumped off the bin. "Where was the law when Angus started fiddling with me? Where was the law tonight when that sod was gross with me? Bruce, the law isn't protection for me. Nor for any woman for that matter. It doesn't deter grubby men from doing what they've decided to do."

She went to walk away.

"Don't go Holly. Don't go off angry. I'm sorry for not understanding. I'm sorry that you've had a rough time. You really don't have to do this. You can go and report whoever it was tonight."

"Bruce, I can't. Word gets around. Many of my regulars are part of the same circle. They are not loners with dirty secrets. They talk to each other. If I lose my customers I'm screwed." Holly took a breath, looked at Bruce and laughed. "Screwed – that's worthy of you, that is!"

Bruce was relieved the atmosphere had lightened.

"Look I'm glad I saw you tonight. I've been wanting to ask you if on one of your Sunday afternoons off you'd like to come to my place for tea?"

"What? Tea at the Vicarage, meet the parents. Bruce are you mad?"

"Not with them there. They go away for the weekend every six weeks – part of a grand plan to keep my father sane. And anyway, it's a Manse not a Vicarage."

"Well pardon me!" Holly curtseyed. "Cucumber sandwiches with the crusts cut off. Do you serve tarts?"

"Holly, please don't mess around. I don't mean like a date – just as a friend."

"Friends. Is that what we are? It's kind Bruce, really it is. Let me think about it."

She walked off. Bruce watched her go waiting for her trademark nonchalant wave. Holly stopped, turned around and smiled. Her eyes glistened. Looking back Bruce would remember thinking it was as though someone had turned on the Christmas tree lights. "Thanks Bruce. You're a decent man."

"Oh Holly. Before you go. I've got a really important question to ask you."

"Not now Bruce, not now."

Chapter 18

May 18th

£70 – shitty, shitty week. TC gross, hurt me. He's changed. Frightens me every time. A-M has promised she'll have knife by next week. Should make me feel safer, though can't really imagine using it.

Saw B for first time in weeks. Surprised me in a car when I was upset, was sweet, too sweet – I nearly told him stuff I shouldn't. He's kind but totally unrealistic – wants me to go to tea at his place.

Nice letter from Auntie Sally. Wanted me to know mum's news. They are thinking of selling up and moving to Spain. Further the better.

Took the bus into Burnham Beeches, the green of the leaves looks so fresh. Love those woods but massive ants – will go back.

Mustn't miss clinic next week.

Chapter 19

Life at the Manse had settled down. For a few weeks Bruce had sensed that he and his parents were tip-toeing round each other. It was the type of large Edwardian house in which it was very easy for people to find their own space. Bruce came in and out at different times according to his shift pattern and his parents had clearly decided not to quiz him on how his work was going. There was no discussion about spiritual issues and his mother offered no further news bulletins on his erstwhile fiancée.

Although Bruce was grateful for this uneasy truce he also regretted that communication with his parents which once had been refreshingly open was now guarded and stilted. On reflection, he realized that this pattern had begun when he and Jenny had started to date. Secrecy was not something that could be restricted to one part of life. It quickly spread and became the norm, much like the invasive Russian ivy growing up the side wall.

One Saturday he found himself having a light supper of cheese on toast with his parents on the patio. Hannah and Sarah were away on a residential weekend with the church youth group. Bruce welcomed the chance to put the relationship with his parents on a more positive footing.

"I'll tell you what Dad, here's something you'll be interested in".
His father looked up from his copy of The Methodist Recorder, grateful to be distracted from reports of denominational concerns and decline.

"I had my first car chase and drink-drive arrest last week."

"Why didn't you tell us?" asked his mother indignantly.

"I'm telling you now, aren't I, if you'll let me!" His mother raised her hands in apology.

"It was just gone mid-night. Things were a bit quiet and I was sitting in that lay-by near the junction on the Beaconsfield Road. A dark blue Jag jumped the lights. There was no-one else around, so I thought I'd just pull it over and give the driver a warning. I went after them with my blue light and flashed with my headlights for them to stop. Anyway, they put their foot down and tried to make a dash for it. I knew I'd got no chance of overtaking, so I kept my distance and followed them home."

"You will be careful Bruce won't you. I don't like to think of you speeding along at night."

"Mum, I've been trained, and I said I didn't try to overtake! Shall I go on?"

Chastened his mother nodded and took a mouthful of Welsh rarebit by way of a gag.

"He turned on to the drive of a posh place on the edge of Burnham Beeches, just up from the convent. I pulled up outside and you'll never guess who it was? Well, actually I can't say – but it's a well-known football manager!"

"Seriously? Go on tell me the club."

"No Dad. I can't even do that. But when I approached him he'd obviously decided it had been a mistake to do a runner. He apologized and admitted he had been drinking. I breathalyzed him there on the drive. He wasn't much over the limit, but I cautioned him and took him down to the station. The lads were impressed I can tell you."

"I bet they were. Did you get his autograph?" asked his father.

"No. But it gets better. I had to sit with him for nearly a couple of hours until he could pass another test. We chatted about all sorts of footie stuff. I told him about how the force team has been going. As he left in a taxi he said that although he wished he hadn't been caught he had enjoyed chatting. Providing his case has been dealt with by the new season he is going to bring a team down to play us as part of their pre-season. How about that?"

"We're talking a west London team, aren't we? I bet it's Chelsea."

"Dad, stop fishing. That's all you're getting."

"Well done son. That is a feather in your cap!"

"Yes. It is Dad. Even DCI Collins stuck his head in the locker room and congratulated me. Now that is the ultimate accolade! Although I suspect it has more to do with his beloved West Ham hating this other team."

Called into Question

"I thought you said you were going to let him off with a warning."

"Mum, if he had only jumped the lights I would have, but once he ran for home and turned out to be drink driving I couldn't turn a blind eye, could I? Too many people, especially sportsmen think they can have a skin-full after a game and still drive home. They are just not safe and it's other people they are putting at risk."

"See you are a proper teetotal Methodist at heart."

"Ha, no Dad, only in your dreams! I do care about keeping people safe though. Is that last piece mine?" he asked helping himself as he did so.
"Ooh my hungry boy. You've had a good appetite ever since your first taste of pasta when you were a bambino!" His mother reached across and pinched his cheek. Bruce winced. "What shift are you on next week Brucie? Great aunt Carlotta is over from Italy doing the rounds of the family. She would so love to see you. Knowing what she is like – make sure you are in uniform."

"Mum, she's in her eighties."

"I know darling. But once a *bella donna* always a *bella donna*."

"You should know if anyone does!" chipped in his father, distracted again from his paper.

"Muir Hammond – and you are still a charmer!"

"You pair of love-birds, behave! To answer your question, I am on a split shift next week. Traffic duty at Royal Ascot on three days. Then I am on stand-by for something a bit different over the weekend. I'll try and see the old girl if I can."

"Something a bit different eh? That sounds interesting. Can we know more?" asked his father.

"Yes, it does and no, you can't! The fact that you even ask shows you should know better." With this Bruce got up and headed into the house. Before disappearing inside, he turned. "Thanks for supper. Glad we got to chat."

Horse-racing was one of the few sports that did not appeal to Bruce. However, the prospect of seeing well-to-do women dressed up to the nines at Royal Ascot was attractive compensation. For the first two days of the meeting he had been rostered for good old-fashioned point duty at one of the car park entrances to the west of the course. He remembered how amusing he had found the practical session at Eynsham Hall during his training. Twenty grown men standing in a circle around the instructor copying his signals had been one of those *pythonesque* moments. At one point when they all had one hand in the air and the sergeant's back was turned Bruce had acted as though he needed to go to the toilet, clutching his groin and grimacing. His fellow recruits across the circle had somehow managed to maintain straight faces throughout his comic performance.

He cut a commanding figure with white gauntlets directing the traffic, standing on the main road and allowing a dozen or so cars at a time to turn in or out of the car park. He drew admiring glances and not a few compliments from women who had clearly started on the champagne at breakfast time.

Day three was the highlight of the festival and from a policing point of view it was a question of all hands to the pumps. It was Ladies' Day and the Royal family would be there in force. The Duke of Edinburgh was expected to drive a coach and horses to the grandstand. The main race of the day was the Gold Cup.

Bruce had been disappointed to discover that his duty that day was to act as driver of a police mini-bus shuttling between Cheston and the racecourse. Chauffeur duties like this bored him and he was particularly sorry to miss the opportunity of casting his eye over the runners and riders in the fashion stakes. There was plenty of banter with the colleagues that he ferried to and from the course.

Towards the end of the day he was driving back in to Cheston with only two WPC's on board when they suddenly came across a hold-up near a major crossroads on the edge of the town. Bruce could see smoke at the junction. There were drivers standing beside their vehicles. Some of them had their hands over their mouths in disbelief.

A man came running towards the van. He was white with shock. "Quick! There's been a smash. People are hurt. Hurt real bad. Thank God you're here. You need to get up there." Bruce put on the blue lights, pulled on to the opposite side of the road and drove to the front of the queue. He was not prepared for the sight that met his eyes. As he approached he had difficulty making sense of the scene before him.

A green Mini was on its' side pinned against the remains of a brick wall by a large silver car, a Rolls Royce. There was broken glass and bricks everywhere. What looked like dirty reddish water from the Mini's radiator was forming a pool on the pavement and in the gutter. Some men were trying to open a door on the shattered car. A group of women on the opposite corner were crying and holding their children close, trying to screen their eyes from the horror. Focussing on the mangled Mini Bruce realized there were people trapped inside.

"Oh my God, there's a baby. Get the baby!" someone shouted. People were screaming as two of the men scrambled on to the bonnet of the Rolls to get closer to the passengers.

Bruce turned to his colleagues. "We need ambulances, fire brigade with cutting equipment and guys from traffic. One of you radio for help and then get the people back down the road. See if you can find the driver of the Rolls. And sort out some eye witnesses. I'll try and see what I can do with the car."

Bruce clambered up onto the silver bonnet alongside the men who were still desperately trying to reach across the twisted door frame of the little car. One turned to look at Bruce as he joined them. There was horror in his eyes. He shook his head. He said nothing.

The other rescuer was desperately trying to reach into the car. "I can't hear the baby anymore. I can't hear it. Got to get it out."

A young man and woman were slumped lifeless against each other leaning down towards the passenger side of the car. The man had taken the full impact of the collision. He had received a traumatic blow to the head. There was blood everywhere. They were pinned by the crumpled frame of the car. Neither of them was moving. Bruce could see immediately they were both beyond reach of help.

"Where's the baby?"

"Behind the woman's seat. In a wicker carry cot. It's gone quiet. I tried to reach it. I tried."

At this point Bruce became aware of approaching sirens. A fire engine and two ambulances arrived almost simultaneously, followed shortly by a car from the Traffic Division.

"Ok guys, come down. Let's see what we can do. You've done all you can."

"No, we haven't. We couldn't reach them. We couldn't reach." The man alongside Bruce was beginning to shake as he spoke.

The fire officer helped Bruce and the distressed rescuer down. His men went quickly to work once they had assessed the chaos. Bruce was aware of a guilty sense of relief at being able to hand responsibility over to others.

He went over to where the WPC's were standing talking to a well-dressed middle-aged woman. He did not tune in to the conversation. He crouched on his haunches and retched in the gutter. Only bile came.

Chapter 20

Bruce sat on the pavement edge for a few moments letting his stomach settle and re-ordering his scrambled senses. He felt numb. A sergeant from Traffic Division had taken control of the situation and was talking to an ambulance man and a doctor. Fire-crew were cutting away part of the side of the stricken Mini. Bruce realized there was now no great sense of urgency.

Another traffic officer was sitting in a patrol car with the driver of the Rolls-Royce. She seemed oblivious to the seriousness of the situation. The sergeant came over to Bruce.

"Sorry lad. Not good news I am afraid. Too late for any of them. Don't blame yourself – you did what you could. Tragic waste. It appears from witnesses that the Roller steamed through red lights doing about 50mph. That little family never stood a chance. They were turning right. The woman's a real old lush – she's way over the limit. I reckon she must have been on the gin and champers all day."

Bruce said nothing as he processed this information. He felt detached.

"I want you to come in the car with us as we take her to your nick. Someone else will bring the van back in a bit."

Bruce nodded. He was relieved not to have to drive again.

Called into Question

Station Sergeant Fleming met them at the back entrance to the station. The traffic sergeant and him clearly knew each other of old. "Alright Phil! Still running the shop here then."

"That's right me old mucker – and you're still road sweeping I see."

"Afraid so. Nasty one this one. Triple fatality RTA. Drunk driver driven her Rolls Royce Silver Shadow right through a Mini. Your lad here did alright by the way."

"Did he indeed."

"Think he could do with a cuppa or something stronger and an early finish."

"I'll see what we can do. We're a bit short with Ascot of course. What's the score with madam here?" Phil Fleming nodded towards the woman sitting in the interview room.

"Lavinia West. She's not with it by a long chalk. Been on the brew all day. Gin and champagne by the sound of it. She says she lives at Gerrards Cross. Failed a breath test at the scene, has been arrested at this stage for dangerous driving and drink-driving. We'll up that to causing death by dangerous later. You'll need to keep her overnight. Magistrates in the morning. I suggest you don't bang her up in a cell till the doctor's seen her and a lawyer's been in."

"Ok, grateful for the advice. Have done this before of course, once or twice.

Called into Question

Just need your mark on this charge sheet and I'll you let get back out on the streets." Fleming didn't take kindly to any advice as to how he should run his personal fiefdom.

The traffic sergeant scribbled a signature on the blank charge sheet Fleming put in front of him and slid it back across the table without saying a word.

He nodded towards Bruce. "Look after yourself son!" and returned to his car in the back yard.

As soon as the traffic officers had driven off, Fleming turned to Bruce. "You can forget any idea of an early finish. We don't do compassionate leave here. So, okay you've seen an accident, it's what we do, comes with the turf. Do you think in the army they excuse people from the battle-field because they've seen some blood or bodies? I don't think so. We're short of people tonight and the last thing I need is having to use someone to guard some fat bitch who can't take her drink. You'll sit with her – treat it as a break if you like. I'll get one of the cadets to make you a cuppa."

"Lady Muck in there can't have anything until the quack has seen her and she's taken another test."

"Yes, Sergeant. And can I just point out it that I didn't ask for time off?"

"You can point out whatever you like Hammond. I'll make my own decisions, thank you very much."

Called into Question

Bruce could see there was little point in having any sort of conversation with Fleming about how he felt about the events of the last couple of hours. The sergeant opened the door and with a nod of his head directed him in to the airless room where Lavinia West was sitting at a table. She was leaning forward resting her head on her arms.

Bruce crossed the room and sat down on an upright chair against the far wall. The dusty venetian blinds stirred slightly in response to the opening and closing of the door. Bruce stretched out his legs and crossed his arms. He studied her, saying nothing. He looked up at the strip-light buzzing slightly overhead. The bodies of a few ill-fated flies littered the opaque plastic shade.

At no point in the events of the last two hours had Bruce spoken to West. He had not seen her charge sheet. She looked in her late fifties or early sixties. Her hair was shoulder length, light brown with expensive-looking highlights. The hat she undoubtedly was wearing at the beginning of this fateful day must be in the car, thought Bruce. She was wearing a blue and turquoise dress with a contrasting short jacket over the top. Even to his untrained eye he could tell it was well-tailored expensive fabric. Rings and a necklace completed the outfit. Everything about it spoke of comfortable wealth. The smartness of her clothes stood in sad contrast to her puffy facial features and general physical appearance. Notwithstanding the efforts of her dress-maker Bruce could see that Lavinia West carried a fair amount of excess "timber" about her body. A glance under the table confirmed this impression. Podgy feet squeezed into designer shoes gave the game away most unattractively.

Bruce maintained his silence. His mind was full of images of the crash. The sergeant had called it an RTA – a Road Traffic Accident but Bruce was aware that this term was becoming more inappropriate with each passing minute as he remembered the sights, sounds and smells from the scene. He ran his tongue over his teeth and swallowed. His saliva had an acidic edge from when he had retched.

Lavinia West sat up in her chair and looked at him. His piercing gaze and brooding silence made her uncomfortable, as Bruce had hoped it would.

"Constable, I would like my handbag returned to me so that I can do my make-up."

Bruce was taken aback. He could not believe what he had heard. "Sorry." he said. "What did you say?"

"I said that I would like my handbag returned. I need to do my make-up. It's been a long day." Her voice was reedy and harsh, clearly a woman who had drunk and smoked all their life. She spoke without emotion. Her speech was still slurred.

Bruce decided to play her along, grimly fascinated by her apparent inability to grasp the seriousness of what had happened.

"How was your day out of interest?" he asked as innocently as he could.

West appeared to welcome the invitation to elaborate. "Well, since you ask, rather fine. Gerald's company had a box, so much more convenient. We had a terrific view all day. Prince Philip driving his coach and horses, he's still so dashing. When Sagaro won the Gold Cup we went wild. Gerald always backs Lester Piggott's mounts. I tell you, he won a bob or two on that!"

Bruce was speechless. He was sitting wondering what it must feel like to be responsible for the death of three fellow human beings and here was this obscene woman waxing lyrical about her fine day at the races. It went through his mind that possibly she was unaware of what had happened. Maybe she had taken a knock to the head in the impact. Perhaps she was in shock. He probed further.

"And how about the end of the day Mrs. West, rather an unfortunate conclusion wouldn't you say."

"Oh that!" Her elbow slipped off the table at this point. She lurched forward against the table awkwardly. "Oops!"

"Yes that. That bump on the way home." Bruce looked at her intently. She tried unsuccessfully to hold his gaze. Bruce took his notebook from the breast pocket of his light blue shirt, glanced at his watch, noted the time and wrote briefly.

"What are you writing? You can't just write down anything I say young man."

"I rather think that I can. If you want to know I am writing down how you have referred to the accident." He was uncomfortable hearing the word from his own lips.

"An unfortunate accident, could happen to anyone. Gerald will pay for any damage. Officer, can you tell me something?" She clearly had to make an effort to concentrate on focusing on Bruce.

"I'll try to. What do you want to know?" Bruce was expecting her to ask after the others involved in the "unfortunate accident".

"My silver lady, my car. Is she badly dented?"

Bruce was outraged. For a moment, he thought he might be sick again as an angry tide of adrenalin surged through his body. Instantly he was on his feet and across the room to the table. He grasped the woman's shoulders and shook her.

"Listen, you fat cow. Is that all you can think about? All you can ask? You've spent the day pouring gin, champagne and God knows what else down your throat, you wipe out an innocent family including a tiny baby," Bruce was shouting right into her face as he shook her, "and all you can ask is whether your fucking car is dented? You revolting rich bitch!"

Lavinia West screamed.

"Let go of me. How dare you talk to me like that? When my lawyer gets here I am going to make an official complaint. I will not be treated like this." The flesh of her turkey neck chins wobbled as she yelled at Bruce.

"You're going to report me? You're mental, you're really mental, do you know that?" Bruce felt something in him was about to snap. He raised his hand to hit her.

"Hammond. No. That's enough". Sergeant Fleming burst into the room. "What the hell do you think you are doing?"

"He assaulted me. He attacked me. He used obscene language." Lavinia West was shouting hysterically.

"Get out of here Hammond."

A WPC and the police doctor appeared at the door. Fleming told them to calm West down while he went to find Bruce.

He found Bruce standing in the shift room, leaning on the coat hooks with his arms outstretched. He was taking deep breaths.

"What the hell do you think you were doing? Have you gone stark raving mad? You laid hands on a woman. You were going to hit her as I came in. You're lucky I heard her screams. And even more lucky I bothered to do something about it."

"Sorry Sarge! Something in me snapped. I lost control. There's a whole family on the way to the mortuary and all she can do is ask for her make-up and the state of her car! What will happen?"

"I don't know. Let's get you out of the way. I suggest you piss off home sharpish. Inspector Middleton will pick up the pieces. But you are in deep shit, up to your neck in it. Off you go. And don't write anything in your pocket book. Understand?"

"Yes Sergeant. Understood."

Chapter 21

Bruce drove home slowly. He felt drained. His rage had died down but like a receding tide it had left the debris of regret and recrimination. The Manse was empty. He remembered his mother having said something about going to a parents' evening at the girls' school. He was relieved to have the house to himself. Helping himself to a large wedge of cheddar and some Ritz biscuits he went up to his room. He showered, dried himself off and put Camel's *The Snow Goose*, on the turntable. He lay on his bed with a towel round his waist and with his hands behind his head. He reached for the rum under the bed. There were only a few dregs left, barely a mouthful. The haunting beginning of the album calmed him at first but as the musical narrative of Gallico's novel gathered pace he felt himself becoming increasingly tense. Two tracks into the second side he jumped up and turned it off. Bruce realized he needed to talk to someone. "Holly's a good listener, she'd be good," he thought. Then he realized that he did not know where she lived and had no means of getting in touch with her.

"Hello Mr. Shaik. Bruce Hammond here. Sorry to ring rather late. I'm very well thank you. Yes, I enjoyed it too, you were very kind. I was wondering if Harpal was home and if so whether I could speak to him please."

Bruce heard Harpal's father call up to him. He could picture him standing at the bottom of the stairs in that comfortable house holding the phone out to his son.
"It's your friend Bruce. He sounds anxious."

"Bruce, how are you? We heard about the accident when we got back to the nick. Terrible. A WPC said you'd been very upset. How do you feel now?"

"I've calmed down a bit, but I could really do with some company. There's no one in at home. I know it's getting late, but could you face going over to Heathrow and getting a coffee together?"

Throughout Bruce's time in the 6th form Heathrow airport had been a regular haunt. A group of his friends would pile into a couple of cars on a Saturday night and go 10-pin bowling at the Airport Bowl before going on to the airport itself. They would sit in Terminal 3 chatting over coffee into the early hours. There was something particularly exciting about sitting in futuristic surroundings hearing announcements about departures to far-off exotic destinations. For young people dreaming of escaping from their parents and striking out for new horizons it was the ideal location.

"Yeah sure, Bruce. I think that sounds like a good idea. I'll drive. Pick you up in about fifteen minutes if that's ok?"

"Thanks. Are you sure you don't mind driving?"

"I wouldn't have offered if I did, would I? See you soon."

As he replaced the phone in his father's study, Bruce recalled one of his father's sayings. "Say what you mean and mean what you say." He couldn't remember where it came from, but he reflected that, apart from the exception of his liking for white girls, Harpal Shaik was not one for playing games. You knew where you stood with him. Bruce wished sometimes that he could be freer from the social games that English politeness dictated to him.

Good as his word, a quarter of an hour later Harpal pulled on to the Manse's large gravel drive in his racing green MGB sports car. It was his pride and joy. One evening in the spring when they had finished a 2-10pm shift they had raced each other from Cheston police station to the bridge over the Thames at the bottom of Eton High Street. Bruce had been proud of holding off his friend on that occasion. A re-match had been in the offing.

Bruce folded himself into the car and they headed east towards Heathrow.

"Thanks for this."

"That's ok." said Harpal cheerfully, "Glad to be of assistance. I did wonder whether you might have phoned Gareth or even a certain young lady."

"Gareth and his missus are on their annual summer pilgrimage back to the land of his fathers and to be honest I don't know how to get in touch with Holly. I don't even know her surname. Any case she's probably," Bruce hesitated.

"Working?" offered Harpal.

"Yes working." Bruce's initial attempts at brightness evaporated.

"Proud to be third choice then!" Harpal said with a light laugh.

They drove the rest of the way along the old A4 Great West Road in silence. As they reached the airport Harpal slowed as the two men watched a Pan-Am Boeing 747 lumber into the air heading west.

"Wow. They are amazing, aren't they? I don't know how they stay up."

"Nor me." said Harpal turning his attention back to the road. "I remember seeing one of the first fly over our school in 1970. We were playing cricket. The batsman stopped the bowler half way through his run-up. We all just stood gaping at the sky – even our sports teacher."

"I'd love to fly on one someday." said Bruce wistfully.

"I'm sure you will my friend. I'm sure you will."

They parked and went into Terminal 3, ordered two coffees and settled down at a table. As they did so a well-spoken woman announced over the public-address system that British Airways was pleased to announce that its' flight to Delhi was ready for boarding.

"The only time we flew from here it was still BOAC." said Harpal.

"When was that?" asked Bruce.

"Must have been three years ago. We went back to Nairobi for my grandmother's funeral. Now tell me what happened earlier."

Bruce took a sip of coffee, glanced out of the window at a VC-10 taxi-ing towards the runway and then began to recount the events of the day. He spoke hesitantly at first and then after a while he gathered pace almost to the point of gabbling. Harpal let him talk without interruption, listening quietly.

"And then she asked for her make-up bag and wanted to know whether her car was badly damaged. That just tipped me over the edge. I felt like there was a volcano in me waiting to erupt. And then it did!" Bruce paused. For a moment, it looked as though he had finished and did not intend to say anything more.

"Is that it?" asked his friend. "What did you do?"
Bruce pursed his lips and put a hand to his mouth. He shook his head a couple of times and looked out of the window. He looked back at Harpal, making and holding eye contact but no words came.

"Better out than in, I think Bruce." Harpal encouraged gently.

Bruce inhaled deeply. He had been fidgeting with a plastic spoon as he spoke. Suddenly the spoon broke in his hands. The dam had given way.
A tear formed in his eye and then rolled slowly down his cheek on to the table. Others followed. Harpal reached across and momentarily grasped Bruce's wrist. "Go on." he urged.

Called into Question

"I just lost it. I went over to her and I shook her by the shoulders. I shouted at her, I swore, and I was going to hit her. That's when Fleming came in. Good job he did. I lost control, simple as that. I felt she deserved it. I don't know what came over me." Bruce looked down, gathered up the pieces of plastic spoon and put them in the ash tray in the middle of the table.

"I think I know what came over you and it's far from simple." said Harpal with a kindly smile. "There is no way you should have been left in that room with her. You were in shock. What you'd seen was horrendous and you'd had no chance to express it to anyone. The Traffic Sergeant was spot on. You should have been sent home."

"But Harpal, Fleming was right, the military don't take a time out at the first sight of blood, do they? You remember Eynsham Hall. They used to wind us up to see if we'd break. If you are emotionally brittle you're a liability. No wonder they kicked people off the course. It's no good, I'll have to jack it in. I'll resign in the morning, if I still have a choice by then!"

"Hold on, hold on. Now is not the time to be making hasty decisions. Be kinder to yourself Bruce. Take a bit of time. Ok fair enough, you've made a mistake but at least wait and see what Inspector Middleton has got to say about it."

Bruce sat silently for a while. He picked up the two sugar cubes from his saucer and slowly unwrapped them. He dropped them into his cup; they splashed in the remains of his cold coffee. Eventually he spoke.

"Yup," he sighed, "you're right. The inspector will want to see me tomorrow anyway. He may make my decision for me!"

"Knowing Middleton, somehow I doubt he will. At least sleep on it eh? There's nothing else you can do now."

"Thanks, Harpal. Appreciate it. I doubt I'll sleep. My dad has one of his sayings, "If you can't sleep don't count sheep, talk to the Shepherd.""

"Pardon, what does that mean?" Harpal looked puzzled.

"Sorry, the shepherd thing is Jesus. It's his funny way of saying better to pray than worry."

"Ok. Well whatever helps. But I didn't think you were much of a one for praying and that stuff."

"No, you're right. I'm not. Thanks again. Can we head back if that's ok with you?"

Chapter 22

Bruce knocked on the door of Inspector Middleton's office. He was summoned in. He had not slept. By the time he had got in from his trip to the airport it had been approaching midnight. He had jotted some notes down in an exercise book he kept in his room. He did this on the basis that although he had been told not to write up his pocket book he knew it might be important to have some relatively fresh memory of all that had happened.

In the morning, he told his father that he had had to deal with a difficult car crash. However, he mentioned neither the deaths nor his subsequent behaviour. He had come to no fresh conclusion about what he should do and hoped the scheduled meeting with the Inspector would prove decisive.

Bob Middleton opened the conversation in a business-like and formal way. "So here we are again PC Hammond! Trying to find a way to tidy up an awkward situation involving your good self. I understand from a number of those also involved in the incident yesterday that you acquitted yourself well at the scene of the accident. Apparently, you took control appropriately, directed people well and put yourself at some risk attempting to assist the casualties."

"Sir. I don't think I was at risk really."

"Well that is not what the fire-officer's report says. It was possible that the Mini could have gone up in flames at any point. The fuel pipe was severed and petrol was spilling all over the place."

"Honestly, I wasn't aware of that at the time. I simply wanted to reach the couple and their baby."

"Most commendable Hammond, the stuff of heroes. Unfortunately, our problem concerns what happened afterwards, doesn't it Hammond."

"Yes sir."

"Last time we sat here chatting like this it was clearly a mess of someone else's making but this time it doesn't look that way from where I am sitting. Are you going to tell me otherwise Hammond?"

"No sir, I am not. I can only apologize. I'm really sorry that I lost my temper. I know I'll have to resign." Bruce spoke with his head bowed and his hands in his lap.

"I'll pretend I did not hear that last comment. I don't want us to be hasty here. It's still early days but I would be interested to hear what you think you have learned from yesterday?" Middleton arranged three or four sheets of paper on the desk in front of him as he spoke. Bruce glanced across the desk at them. They appeared to be typed reports.

Bruce took his time before answering. "I think I realize now that I am not as controlled as I like to think."

Inspector Middleton nodded. "Have you had problems with your temper, outside of work? At home or in your other personal relationships?"

Bruce was taken aback that his superior was going to probe like this. "Well, like most people I guess I have my moments at home. I have raised my voice to my parents and my sisters on occasions."

"Like most people? I got the distinct impression from our previous meeting that you thought you were not like most people. You were different – in fact something of a crusader for doing things the right way. You say you have "raised your voice?" Is that a euphemism Hammond? I assume you know what one of those is?"

"Yes sir, I do." Again, Bruce hesitated. "Yes, I have lost my temper a few times recently."

"The thing is Bruce. I have got to decide today how we play this. A key factor in that decision is whether I think you are a liability to the force. If I conclude that you are unable to control yourself I will recommend that you be dismissed from the force. Do you understand?"

"Yes sir, I do." Bruce was beginning to feel that he almost would have preferred an old school rollicking than this calculated, reasoned approach. He felt that was what he deserved. He craved punishment.

"Are there any extenuating circumstances or excuses you want me to bear in mind?"

"No sir, none." Bruce responded crisply and without hesitation.

"Are you sure about that? There is a view held by some that you should not have been expected to sit in with the prisoner." Bob Middleton looked at Bruce closely as he waited for his response.

"No sir. That's kind of people, whoever they are, but I think I ought to have been able to maintain my control and act in a professional manner."

"Do you indeed. Well for what it's worth I agree with you. I am glad to hear you say that. It does however lead me on to a further question. I will be very interested in your answer."

Bruce shifted uncomfortably on his chair. He wondered where Middleton was going with his questioning.

"What I want to know is this PC Hammond. How do you think your treatment of Lavinia West differs from the treatment of those prisoners that you raised with me last time we spoke together?" Having put his question Inspector Middleton folded his arms and leaned back in his seat. He clearly expected a considered response.

Bruce had spent his sleepless hours turning over many questions in his mind; some were of a personal nature and others were more philosophical. Harpal's parting comment about him not believing in prayer had also got under his skin to an extent that had surprised him.

"I've been asking myself the same question sir."
Middleton opened his hands in an inviting gesture, "the floor's all yours."

"I know it is inexcusable, like I said earlier. I know it doesn't look good, but I do think it is different. Some of the beatings I have seen or heard about are gratuitous, just for the sake of it. Some of them are even pre-planned and others are, I don't know." He hesitated and looked past the inspector towards the window as though seeking inspiration. He continued, "Are some are sort of rough justice, to teach a lesson. I remember when I used to work as a porter at the hospital in my holidays; three of the lads gave a kiddy fiddler who was brought in to A and E a terrible beating. No-one seemed to bat an eye-lid, and the guy himself didn't make a complaint."

"Are you trying to tell me that there was any thought behind what you did last night?"

"No sir, not for one moment. I just snapped. I do remember thinking as I sat in silence watching her that she deserved a good slapping, but I didn't decide to do that. It's not an excuse but a whole load of emotion and anger, most of it to do with the crash, built up and built up and then, like I said, I just exploded!"

The inspector nodded. "I remember you telling me very articulately that once we take the law into our own hands, even if in the mistaken belief that we are upholding the law, we are under-mining it. I told you to hold on to that. Do you remember?"

Bruce nodded.

"I happen to think that your explanation of what happened shows a fair degree of self-awareness. What is more I think the distinction you have made between the different types of physical mistreatment is accurate. However, here is my problem. Motives and emotions are difficult to prove, especially in a court of law. You assaulted Mrs. West, plain and simple, and you are very fortunate that unintentionally Sgt. Fleming came to your rescue. Frankly, I am surprised he did, but be that as it may. If you had hit her I suspect, we would be having this conversation under caution in the very same interview room."

Bruce felt queasy as he listened. He sensed the exchange was reaching its logical conclusion. He tried to brace himself for what he was about to hear.

Bob Middleton continued. "The distinction you have made would be impossible to uphold in a court or when facing the press. The bare facts shout too loudly, they drown out any subtle nuances. Do you understand?"

Bruce nodded again. Inwardly he was trying not to flinch.

"Did it occur to you that Mrs. West might want to press charges against you? To do so would not protect her from the due process of law surrounding her case but would cause big trouble for you. What is more, if she had a certain sort of lawyer, your actions might even have under-mined the prosecution's case to an extent. All in all, not very clever."

"Are the West's going to make a complaint against me sir?"

"No Hammond, remarkably, they are not. You can thank Mr. West for that shred of good news on a bad day. It turns out that Gerald West has been tearing his hair out for some years in attempts to convince his wife that her drinking was out of control. When he arrived with the lawyer, Lavinia West predictably started shouting the odds about the way you had treated her. She made a great fuss and a lot of noise until her husband got hold of her and said, and I quote, "Serves you right you stupid, stupid woman. Shame he didn't slap you. May be if I had shaken you up a few years ago three people would still be alive." To say it took the wind out of her sails would be an understatement. She accepted the charge, is going to plead guilty and was released on bail first thing this morning."

Bruce was shocked at this turn of events.

"So, you see PC Hammond, being a successful police officer is rather like being a football manager – not only do you have to be good, you also have to be lucky! And it appears that you are one lucky young man. Anything else you want to say?"

Bruce shook his head. "Thank you, sir."

"Ok. Dismissed. Go and get a cuppa and then report to your shift."

Bruce headed across the back yard of the station towards the canteen building. As he was taking the stairs up to the first floor two at a time he nearly bumped into Detective Chief Inspector Ted Collins.

"Whoa there. If it isn't my favourite golden boy who fell to earth. Always in a hurry I see." Collins's voice always had a slightly nasal sneering edge to it. "I hear you are finally beginning to show signs of progress. Cottoning on to how we do things round here. They tell me you finally roughed up a prisoner Hammond. Well done. Trouble is you don't appear to have worked out quite how it works. Let me explain." Collins had his arms out barring the way.

"We are very particular about who we get a little physical with. You can always have a pop at the Paddies, the winos, the blacks and the queers. Do you get my drift Brucie? In other words, people who can't hurt us back. We don't slap people with money, good connections and decent lawyers; for obvious reasons, but don't let me discourage you. We all have to start somewhere." He stepped aside with a flourish. "Carry on PC Hammond, enjoy your cucumber sandwich or are you having the humble pie today?"

Bruce went to move on. "Just one more thing, Hammond. How's it going with the tartlet? Are you giving her one yet?"

Chapter 23

"Right, who'd like the first pieces of eggy-bread?" asked Sophia Hammond brightly.

Sarah and Hannah jumped up from the table and held their plates out towards their mother who was standing at the oven with a large frying-pan in her hand. "Steady, form a queue. Bruce would you like some?"

He was just about to say he'd make do with his normal piece of toast and mug of coffee when he had second thoughts. "Yes please, I'd love some if my greedy sisters leave any for the workers in the family!"

"Hey, that's not fair. I'm not greedy." squealed Hannah.

"No, I can see that from the three pieces of eggy-bread on your plate."

"It's ok, I am doing plenty. I want to use up this box of eggs. Oh, it is such a treat having you here for breakfast with us. It's like the old days when you all got ready for school together."

"Why are you going in to work late today?" inquired Hannah.

"If you must know, I've been put on a three-day attachment to a department called the Collator's Office."

"What's a Collator?" asked Sarah.

"It's someone who keeps all the files we have about people in order and who sifts through reports that come to the station in different ways. They look at it all and pass on what they decide is important or useful."

"Sounds like an Intelligence Officer in the army." said his mum looking up from watching the next batch of bread dipped in egg sizzling in the pan.

"Well, yes, that's it really. They are a local intelligence officer." agreed Bruce.

"Do they have to be super clever?" asked Hannah writing her initials in tomato sauce on her bread as she did so.

"Not really," replied Bruce, "just very organized and methodical."

"Give me your plate Bruce, these pieces are ready now. I just think it's lucky that this placement has come up so soon after you had to deal with that terrible accident."

Bruce sighed. "Yes, Mum. Very lucky, isn't it?"

When Bruce had gone to his locker at the end of his shift the previous day he had found one of Inspector Middleton's notes sellotaped to his locker.
"Bruce, I hope you'll take some time to think about your future and not jump into a decision you may regret later. I have arranged for you to spend the next

three days on attachment to the Collators' Office. As you know, the Collators normally work 9-5. I hope you find the experience interesting and helpful. Insp R J M."

Set up for the day by his mother's cooked breakfast and feeling slightly more cheerful than he had the previous morning, Bruce cycled in to Cheston. He enjoyed doing this on summer mornings. A section of his route took him along a path beside the Thames. Two swans were teaching their cygnets how to negotiate the wash of cabin cruisers.

The Collators' Office was a square room adjacent to the Interview room. Back to back in the centre were two banks of filing cabinets. They were dark green, and the drawers were postcard size. On the top were two metal trays marked *Info In* and *Info Out*. Officers were encouraged to write any information that might be of wider interest on pro forma and leave these in the appropriate tray. On three walls were large pin-boards. It was expected that those going out on patrol would spend time regularly in this treasure trove of information. Bruce had made it part of his daily routine to visit the room, so he was no stranger to the place when he went in that morning. The Collator on duty was a PC called Ian who was approaching retirement. He welcomed Bruce warmly, appreciative of company and recognizing him as a regular "customer". He made no reference to the recent events that had brought Bruce to his small but strategic department. However, Bruce sensed Ian had been fully briefed.

"I'm glad to have an extra pair of hands to be honest Bruce. I have recently updated about 100 CRO cards and they need to be re-filed if you can face that.

The thing is I have got a little behind ever since Geoffrey Rollinson retired."

Bruce was happy to oblige. In his short time stationed at Cheston he had become fascinated by the hundreds of record cards. Each one told a story, usually a tragic one of the unraveling of a life. In his first week, he had picked out the record cards of a pair of tramps who had been regular visitors to the Manse. They were both ex-servicemen, alcoholics whose addiction had cost them dear. It had been poignant to see the mug shot photos from their first arrests and then to see subsequent ones that catalogued their physical and mental decline over the ensuing years. Both men had done gardening for his parents when they were "well" in return for food, clothing and occasional lodging in an outhouse. Most of their offences were for shop-lifting and being drunk and disorderly. Bruce spotted a pattern of "assault on police" happening in the late autumn resulting in jail terms over the coldest part of the winter. He had been shocked to find on one of the cards among the many petty crimes a conviction for indecent assault. This had resulted in a much longer sentence. Bruce wondered what his mother would say if she knew her Christian kindness had unwittingly left her daughters in a vulnerable situation.

Ian was a chatty individual who welcomed the novelty of having a colleague working with him. "Have you heard that Gareth Williams is going to become the other Collator? He kept an eye on you when you first arrived didn't he?"

Bruce nodded. With such recall Ian was plainly well-suited to his role. "I hadn't heard that, but I think he is ready to give up his beat. When does he start?"

"Tomorrow actually, when he comes back to work after his break."

"Ah yes, the annual pilgrimage home." Bruce was encouraged by the prospect of talking to his steady mentor.

Ian went for his coffee break leaving Bruce minding the phones and the telex machine in the corner. Bruce took his opportunity to open one of the two drawers containing the criminal records of women. Comparing the space allocated for the respective sexes underlined the fact that men were more liable to criminality than women. Either that, or women were more adept at going undetected!

When Ian returned Bruce decided to broach a subject that had been bothering him in the same way that a small stone in a shoe causes discomfort until it is removed. On his first visit to this office he had been struck by the fact that one of the notice boards was covered exclusively with pictures of black Afro-Caribbean youths.

"Ian, do you mind if I ask you something. Something that's been on my mind ever since I began here?"

"Fire away. What is it?"

"Well, it seems strange that there is a whole wall given over to pictures of black young men. If that is pretty much the last thing we look at before we go out on the beat looking for local criminals, it's no surprise that black

Called into Question   171

youngsters complain they get stopped more often than white guys. What's the thinking behind it?"

"Your friend Harpal asked me that a few months ago. Did he ask you to ask?"

"No, he's never mentioned it. We've never discussed it."
"I'm surprised he hasn't then. He was quite worked up about it, especially when I told him the reason why."

"Which is?"

The older PC looked awkward. I was instructed to put all the pictures up by DCI Collins. He said it would be useful because "all black people look alike to us whites. Those weren't his precise words."

"I can imagine. Wow, no wonder Harpal was cross. That's outrageous. You only have to glance at this notice board itself to see that clearly isn't true."
"I know Bruce, I know." Ian looked at his feet. "You've been here long enough by now to know you can't really have a discussion with Ted Collins."

"No, you're right there. Anyway, thanks for telling me. I wasn't having a go at you personally and I doubt that Harpal was either."

"I know. It's just the way it is I'm afraid."

* * * * *

That evening Bruce, Harpal and two others of the single men on their shift had arranged to meet up in Windsor for a drink at a pub overlooking the river near the picturesque race-course. The evening was full of good-hearted banter, discussions about the forthcoming Ashes cricket series with Australia and speculation about the social lives of various WPC's. By the end of the evening the company combined with the effects of a few pints of Guinness had lightened Bruce's mood.

"Are you coming into Windsor for a kebab?" asked Harpal.

"No, I'll pass on that, I'll head back now. Thanks guys, a good evening." Bruce gave a theatrical salute as he turned towards the car park. He set off home but when he reached a large roundabout on the edge of the town he drove past the exit for his village. Instead he turned on to the dual carriage-way for Cheston.

He parked his car and walked the last three hundred yards to the parade of shops. A quick glance confirmed that the Chinese take-away was still serving. He walked round the back, treading carefully so as not to make too much noise on the gravel. He was not quite sure at what point in the evening he had decided to come here. He recognized it was a wild and possibly unwise impulse but having come this far there was no point going back now. He was in luck. Most of us are creatures of habit and Holly was no exception.

She was sat on her normal bin tucking into a couple of spring rolls. A small cup of sweet and sour sauce was balanced precariously on the next bin.

Called into Question

"Hello there, what's this then? Lunch break?"

Holly was startled and jumped off the bin, knocking the sauce to the ground in the process.

"Thanks a bunch Bruce. What the hell are you doing creeping up on me like that? You gave me a fright."

"I can see that," he said looking at the spreading pool of glutinous sauce. The mini-tidal wave absorbed dust in its flow. "Sorry. I was on my way home from a few drinks with Harpal and a couple of the other lads."

"Oh good. Where did you go?"

"That old pub near the racecourse."

Holly looked at Bruce quizzically. "Got a little lost, did you? This isn't exactly the scenic route home."

Bruce looked embarrassed and kicked himself for not really having thought through his story.

"I was peckish. Needed some post-drink soakage."

"So, you thought you'd come via your favourite Chinese."

Bruce raised his hands in admission. "Ok you've caught me out. I hoped I might bump into you."

"Well I am flattered. How are you now after the accident? Have you calmed down?"

"Who told you about that?"

It was Holly's turn to look embarrassed. "The guy who sells The Evening Echo outside the Railway Station mentioned it."

"Did he indeed?" Bruce was not surprised that the wider public knew about the accident, but it bothered him that news of his outburst had got out. For a few moments, this revelation interrupted his train of thought.

"Sorry Bruce. Have I said the wrong thing? Do you want this spring roll? We're right out of sauce – thanks to the local snooper!"

Bruce climbed onto the bin and took the remaining roll. "Come and sit down again." He shuffled across to make room for Holly.

"No, I'm fine thanks. I ought to be off in a moment."

"Was it something I said?" asked Bruce hoping he had masked the disappointment he felt.

"Not really. I've got to meet someone I'm afraid, but also, I can see you've had a bit to drink. I don't want you to say or do something you might regret. I think you've had more than your fair share of incident and excitement for one week."

"Hold on just a minute Holly. That's fair enough. I did want to say something, and it is not a spur of the moment thing." Bruce looked at Holly. She looked apprehensive. "Don't worry I'm not going to propose."

"Good, that *would* be an awkward moment."

"Seriously. The other week when I said we were friends, you looked uncomfortable." Holly went to speak but Bruce stopped her. "Hear me out."

She nodded.

"I do think of you as a friend, but I realized I don't even know where you live. When it all went pear-shaped on the day of the accident I wanted to get in touch, because I think you are a great listener. I didn't have a clue how to contact you."

Holly smiled at Bruce. "Why not address a postcard to Holly c/o the Bins behind the Chinky?"

"Holly!" Bruce was exasperated. "I am trying to be serious here."

Called into Question 176

"I know you are and it makes me feel uncomfortable."

"Look I just wanted you to know I value your friendship. I'm not after anything. My family is away in a fortnight's time and I'd love to treat you to a proper Sunday tea."

Holly hesitated for a moment or two. Bruce knew by now the importance of giving her space to process a suggestion or question. He said nothing.

"What's the address Bruce?" she asked, looking away as she did so.

"The Manse, Beech Gardens, Flatley. Does that mean you'll come?"

"Yes, I will. That's kind of you. Thank you."

"I'll come and pick you up if you like."

"No thanks. I'll be fine to make my own way there."

"Great! See you then if not before."

Holly was about to head to her next appointment when she stopped and turned. Bruce expected the customary wave. "If I am coming to tea, I suppose I had better let you know my name. It's Brewer." And with that she turned and was gone. Bruce licked his fingers and wiped his chin before heading back to his car.

Called into Question

Chapter 24

June 19th

Think I've been stupid. B surprised me again last night. I knew he'd been upset, let my guard down. May have given things away – not sure. If I have, it will be a sort of relief. I felt sorry for him. He's asked me to go to his place when his people are away. I've said yes and told him my surname. What an idiot. Won't I ever learn? Will put it off. He'll be disappointed.

A-M got me the knife. I love it. Mother of pearl handle – reminds me of the dish my dad used his studs and cuff-links. It's very sharp. I cut myself on my forearm trying it out. Very clean. Never thought I'd own a knife. Thinking about where to keep it.

TC in strange mood – planning something. Uneasy – I have a bad feeling about this.

Chapter 25

Next day in the Collators' office Bruce surprised himself by taking the earliest opportunity to flick through the cards in the "B" section of the women's records. "Baines, Barker, Bradbury, Brewster." No Brewer. He was relieved.

Later in the day Bruce was in the middle of a deep conversation with Gareth Williams about his future when they were interrupted by the arrival of DC Rob Finlay. Bruce had had very little contact with him since they had arrested the black youth at the beginning of his short-lived CID placement.

"Hammond, there you are. DCI Collins wants you upstairs for a briefing at two o'clock. Don't be late."

"Right thanks Finn."

"Don't thank me. I wouldn't have you within a hundred yards of our department." Finlay did not wait around for a response.

Bruce and Gareth looked at each other.

"They say that like dogs, Detective Constables get like their owners." said Gareth wryly. "Do you know what that's about?"

"Yes, I think it's about a special operation. They want some of us uniform boys on it. Although I'd assumed in the light of all this hassle over the

Called into Question

accident I wouldn't be wanted." said Bruce.

"They probably need some fresh, young legs to do a spot of chasing. I can't think why they didn't choose me!" said the Welshman patting his ample belly. "I was a nippy wing three-quarter in my day. Make sure you look after yourself. Remember what they say, a dead hero is no good to anyone."

"Well thanks for that cheery advice."

Half an hour later Bruce was sitting perched on the corner of a desk in the main open plan CID office. Harpal Shaik was next to him.

"Collins must be desperate if he's chosen both of us. We're hardly flavour of the month with him!" Bruce said to his friend.

Harpal shot Bruce a knowing look and said under his breath, "Either that, or he's setting us up in some way."

"When David and Jonathan there at the back have finished whispering love messages to each other, I'll begin." Some in the room turned to look at Bruce and Harpal. Others sniggered at DCI Collins's snide comment. "Have you two finished?"

Harpal nodded.

Ted Collins spent the next fifteen minutes explaining how this special operation would work. CID had been keeping a well-known local criminal under surveillance. The man was known to be the number two to a much bigger fish, a serious gangland player called Peter Brady. He had moved out to the Algarve a couple of years before, ostensibly for the sun but also to escape the attention of the Met. Police's Organized Crime Unit. The local man kept an eye on Brady's prostitution and protection rackets for him. Recently it had been rumoured that the gang was diversifying into the lucrative drugs scene. Ted Collins had heard via personal contacts in Spain that Brady had slipped back into the country within the last fortnight. He was believed to be staying in a large rented property in Burnham, within easy reach of the M4 junction to the west of the town.

Collins had also been informed that the Met. Police Flying Squad intended to raid the premises within the next week. He had decided to steal a march on them by beating them to it. The dozen officers in the room including a WPC and a dog handler were the team he had chosen to surprise Brady and three of his associates. The plan was to storm the house shortly after midnight. Collins suspected that Brady may be preparing to leave the country via a small private airfield near Basingstoke that he often used. He ended his briefing in the style of a football manager giving a half-time team talk.

"I am not going to have those smug buggers from the smoke getting a result on our patch. We are going in hard and fast. I want each of you to bring your A-game to the party." Bruce tried not to smile at the Churchillian style and dramatic mixed metaphors.

Called into Question

Bruce and Harpal had been given the task of shutting off what had been identified as a potential escape route. They were evidently on the team because they were grudgingly recognized as being the two fittest officers in the station. Collins made it clear that if all went according to plan their services would not be required.

"Any questions?" Collins asked this in such a way as to make it obvious he did not expect any.

The Dog Handler was normally stationed elsewhere and had been brought in specially. He did not know Ted Collins but the question he asked was one that undoubtedly had occurred to most in the room. "Sir, do we expect them to be armed?"

Collins gave him a withering look. "I would have said so if that were the case. My understanding on this occasion is that they are not. When Brady wants shooters, he employs an ex-SAS man. No more questions. We rendezvous here at 11pm!"

On their way out of the briefing Bruce and Harpal were taken to one side by a Detective Sergeant and given more precise details about their role. They were to be in uniform but in an unmarked car, a red Ford Escort had been booked from the car pool. The sergeant gave them a map of the area on which a small unmarked lane had been added in hand. It was the back entrance to the property, was about half a mile long and at one point went under a bridge on a disused railway line. They were to blockade the lane at this point.

Called into Question

"If any of them do make a break for it you are to do whatever it takes to stop them. Oh, and when you get into the area switch from the main radio channel to channel 3 on your car set. Understood."

Bruce and Harpal nodded.

Later that night Harpal drove them to their position. As they approached the entrance to the driveway Bruce looked across at him. "How are you feeling? Nervous?"

"Not really nervous. Just a bit of an edge." Harpal replied. "How about you?"

"Yes, an edge. That's a good way of putting it. It feels a bit like how I feel before a big match or a race. Excited but also slightly uncertain how it will go."

"Well to be honest," said Harpal turning slowly into the lane, "I suspect we are just here as insurance. I'll be very surprised if we are required. I think we'll turn out to be the bridesmaids, dressed in blue."

"What makes you say that?"

"Stands to reason. Collins doesn't like either of us and probably doesn't trust us. He's hardly likely to risk his chance to put one over the London boys by giving us a key role."

"You don't really think we're being set up then?"

"Nothing would surprise me about Collins. But I don't think he'd risk an operation like this over a personal grudge."

"Well, I hope you're right, Harpal. I've not got a good feeling about this."

Harpal drove them slowly towards the bridge using only sidelights. The lane became even narrower at the bridge. It was about fifteen metres high. The brickwork was dark, almost black with a slight sheen finish even after all these years. There was a parapet on both sides about two metres from the top of the grassy embankment.

"Let's forget Collins and his games for the moment. How are we going to play this?" asked Harpal getting out of the car.

The two men stood surveying the scene. Bruce shone his torch inside the tunnel. "I used to play on a bridge like this when I was a kid. We used to pretend it was our castle." He walked through the tunnel and looked at it from the other side. By the time he returned to Harpal at the car he had formulated a plan.

"How about this for an idea? If Brady and his crew come this way almost certainly they will be pursued, so we need to set things up to try and delay them, trapped like rats in a pipe."

"Fair enough. Go on." Harpal could see his friend's brain was working in overdrive.

"So, you park the car, about ten or fifteen yards back from the tunnel just before the lane narrows. That way you can put it into position and block this end just as they think the way is clear."

"Where are you going to be then?" Harpal asked.

"I'll be up on the parapet the other side. There's a pile of old bricks on the slope there. I'll take some with me. They'll be driving at speed. I'll put a couple of those through the windscreen if I can as they go into the tunnel. It should mean that they'll be easy pickings for the lads chasing them." Bruce was clearly benefitting from a surge of adrenalin.

"Sounds reasonable. Of course, we are assuming Collins and the others will be tight on their tails. Could be awkward if not."

"Come on. Even if for some bizarre reason the others are slow in coming it still puts us in a strong position. Have you got a better idea?"

Harpal shook his head.

"Ok then let's do it."

The quietness of the night was suddenly disturbed by the radio set crackling into life. Collins's harsh nasal tone was accentuated by the radio. "All units. Going in ten. Sundance confirm you are in position?"

Harpal picked up the handset. "Sundance affirmative."

"Right then," said Bruce, "you back up a little. I'll grab some bricks and leg it up the other side." He smiled at Harpal. "Good luck to us then."

"Whatever luck is. If it comes down to luck, we'll be in trouble. What will be will be!"

"Cheers. Not a good time to get philosophical." With this Bruce jogged away through the tunnel.

He scrambled up and down the steep embankment three times carrying a few bricks at a time. Then he crouched down, laid his torch and truncheon on the ground on one side and the bricks on the other. As he waited so he became more attuned to the sounds and smells of his surroundings. A light breeze was stirring the treetops. The air was heavy with earthy, woody smells; bracken and wild garlic. He was alert, listening in the stillness for any clue of how things were unfolding at the house. After all the upset and numbing anxiety of recent weeks it felt good to be fully engaged in something, fully alive.

Suddenly, the woodland peace was broken by a loud splintering noise, shouts and a dog barking. There were more shouts and then the chilling unmistakable sound of two gun-shots rang out. "Oh my God," thought Bruce, "they are armed." His skin prickled, he felt the hairs on his neck and arms stand up. His stomach turned.

There were two more shots followed by the sound of a car starting and being driven away at speed. Bruce heard Harpal shout, his voice echoing in the tunnel. "They're coming our way." Through the trees Bruce heard more shouts, the dog barking and other vehicles being started. He could see the beam of headlights getting nearer. Behind him he heard Harpal start the Escort. He took a brick in each hand. He realized that he probably would only get one chance to throw.

The car hurtled into view round a bend in the drive about fifty yards away. Bruce recognized it as an Audi 100; his uncle owned one. The headlights were on full beam and picked Bruce out as he stood and steadied himself to take aim. The car slowed momentarily before accelerating. He took aim and hurled a brick at the driver's side of the windscreen. He was on target. The impact of the brick as it went through the windscreen sounded like an exploding grenade. The car swerved to the right and caught the leading edge of the tunnel brickwork, ripping off the front wing. The car came to a halt in the middle of the tunnel. At this point Harpal turned on the Escort's headlights to dazzle the occupants.

Bruce grabbed his truncheon, wrapping the leather thong at the top round his wrist as he scrambled and slid down the embankment. He could hear shouts, the sound of another car and the barking of a dog getting nearer. As he reached the bottom a short thick-set man ran out of the tunnel. Bruce realized he must be the passenger. Bruce reached to grab him, but the man dodged his grasp and started to run into the woodland along the bottom of the embankment.

"Stop!" shouted Bruce, "you can't get away." The man continued to try and run across the uneven ground, his arms flailing at the undergrowth and small branches in his way. Bruce quickly gained on him. The man was breathing heavily and was clearly unfit. Bruce prepared to tackle him. He was aware of something close behind him. The man stumbled, and Bruce launched himself. As he fell the man twisted round before landing. There was a loud noise. Instantly Bruce felt an extreme stinging, burning sensation at the top of his chest. He landed on the man at the same time as the Alsatian dog pounced, snarling and biting the gunman's arm. Bruce knew immediately that he'd been shot. He couldn't move. He was aware of the dog, of people shouting and then nothing.

Chapter 26

Bruce opened his eyes and tried to focus on the nurse standing beside his bed. "Jenny?" he said quietly. "What are you doing here? Why am I in London?"

"It's okay Bruce. Try not to talk. I'm Fiona, the nurse looking after you. You are in Wexham Park Hospital. You've had an operation, you're doing ok, but you need to rest."

"Sorry, thought you were someone else."

"Don't worry, it's not a problem." said Fiona gently. "Try and rest. Let me know if you are in pain and I'll get the doctor to give you something stronger. You are going to feel rather woozy until the anaesthetic wears off."

Bruce tried to move his right arm but found he could not. His left arm was connected to two drips. "What are these?"

"You have lost a lot of blood, so we are topping up your system. The other is fluid and a pain-killer. Now please try and rest. One of the doctors will come and see you in a while. She will explain what they have done." Fiona plumped up his pillow and checked the drip-lines. "I will be right outside if you need anything. I'll check you regularly."

"Thanks Jen. Love you" he mumbled.

He felt feverish and tired. His body seemed heavy – almost as though it was someone else's that he was watching. He tried to recall what had happened. He remembered being in a wood, running and being chased by a dog. It seemed confusing. He could not make sense of what had happened. After a while he abandoned the struggle, closed his eyes and went to sleep.

He woke three hours later. His head was clearer. He could see he was in a single room. His right arm was heavily bandaged from the elbow upwards and was resting in a metal cradle on the bed. There was a padded dressing across his shoulder and upper chest. Intravenous drips were still connected to his left arm.

"Hello my darling boy. You've slept and slept." His mother, Sophia, got up from a chair and stood beside his bed. His father was with her. She put her hand on his forehead as though to feel his temperature and to soothe him. "Bruce, we've been so worried about you. Thank God you're safe."

His father put his hand gently on top of Sophia's. He had tears in his eyes. "Yes, thank God, we've had so many people praying for you. Are you in pain?"

Bruce looked up at his parents. He remembered how they had stood like this over his bed when he had had his tonsils removed when he was seven. They had bought him a Corgi model car, a blue racing car transporter. It had been the prize model in his collection for years. His parents looked tired but relieved.

"No, I'm not in pain. I still feel rather fuzzy. What time is it?"

"It's seven thirty, son." said his father.

"Morning or afternoon?"

"It's morning darling. They brought you here in the night. We got a phone call about half past two. That nice Inspector Middleton told us you'd been hurt but you would probably be ok. We came here immediately." Sophia sat back in the blue plastic arm chair and folded the blanket she had used during her night-time vigil over her son.

"I was shot, wasn't I? I remember now. I chased someone. I think they tripped and shot me as I dived on them." Bruce frowned with the effort of remembering the events of the night before.

"We don't really know the details, other than you were shot with a handgun. You lost a lot of blood. Apparently, your friend Harpal did a great job. Saved your life." Muir Hammond choked up as he said these last words.

"Oh Bruce, it doesn't bear thinking about. I don't know what I'd have done if we'd lost you. I couldn't bear it. But you're going to be ok." His mother took a handkerchief from her handbag and blew her nose inelegantly.

At this point, Fiona the nurse put her head round the door. "Reverend Hammond. Mrs. Hammond, the doctor wants to have a word with Bruce now to explain what has happened. Perhaps this is a good time to go and get a coffee from the canteen. They will be serving breakfast soon." Bruce's parents took the hint, gathered their things and went in search of the canteen.

"Hello Bruce. I am Doctor Park. Felicity Park, I am the senior Registrar. I work on the team with Mr. Gannon. He is the surgeon who patched you up. You are a lucky young man."

"I don't feel very lucky, to be honest, lying here." said Bruce flatly.

"I guess not. Perhaps lucky isn't the best word." Felicity Park smiled as she spoke. "Nevertheless, you are fortunate. You were shot by a handgun from close quarters. You could have been killed instantly. It appears the bullet entered diagonally near the top of your chest. It nicked the edge of your subscapular artery and left a ragged wound. If it had severed the artery you could have bled to death very quickly. Fortunately for you your colleague PC Shaik seemed to know what he was doing and staunched the bleeding as best he could."

"Harpal, a man of many talents. A good friend to have."

"It would appear so." agreed the doctor.

"Funny, talking about being lucky. One of the last things he and I talked about before this happened was about luck and what it is. I remember he said, "what will be will be."

"There we are then. No doubt you can continue that conversation when he comes and visits you. I know he is keen to see you. Now, in terms of what we have done. My colleague Mr. Gannon operated to stop the bleeding and to repair the artery as best we could. He has also repaired the entry and exit wounds. You have some muscle damage in your shoulder. That will be painful for some months but in time you should be able to build up the muscles around the site. I imagine you will regain most of the movement in your shoulder, providing you work at the exercises a physio will give you."

"Thank you, doctor. Please pass on my thanks to your colleague."

"You can do that yourself when you see him later today or tomorrow. Again, you were indeed fortunate in that before becoming consultant here Mr. Gannon was a senior registrar in Belfast from the start of the Troubles. He is one of the leading experts in the treatment of bullet wounds."

"Anyway, lucky or not, I am very grateful. Doctor how long do you think I am going to be in hospital?"

"Hopefully not too long. Possibly four or five days. We will want to see that you don't have a reaction to the repair we have done. There may be some damage to the median nerve which we will only be able to assess when the swelling has gone down. Also, because you did lose a lot of blood there is no harm in us keeping an eye on you for a few days. Talking of which you should know that your superior officers have placed one of your colleagues outside. They are there to protect you from unwanted guests, including journalists. You are quite a news item. National news no less."

"Oh, I hadn't thought about that."

"I am not surprised," said the doctor, "you've not had much chance to think about anything. I want you to rest. Don't be surprised if you have a delayed reaction to the shock of being shot. Lots of people do suddenly feel wobbly and all over the place emotionally. It's quite normal and it will pass."

"Ok, thanks for the warning."

"Later today or tomorrow I understand a colleague from CID will come and take a statement from you. Presumably he or she will be able to tell you more about what happened."

"It will be a *he*, doctor, you can bank on that."

Bruce's parents came back from the canteen. "Now we know you are ok we'll head back. The girls will be glad to hear the news." said his father.

"We'll come back at 2pm when visiting hours start. What would you like me to bring? Shall I bring some of my special pasta?"

"No, mum, that's kind but I'll be fine with the food here. Pyjama bottoms would be good. Not sure what I can get over my top with all these dressings and gubbins. Something to read would be nice. No offence – but nothing religious."

Bruce glanced at his father as he said this. Muir Hammond could not hide a momentary look of disappointment.

"Don't worry Dad. I'm not an atheist. I've just got lots of questions at the moment."

"Nothing wrong with questions, son. You know that. If you don't question in life you don't grow. See you later. Try and rest."

"Bye Dad, Bye Mum. Love you guys."

His parents left the room. He heard his mother sob as soon as she was out of the room. She had struggled to hold things together.

Bruce dozed fitfully throughout the morning. He found it hard to lie comfortably, restricted as he was by the cradle, dressings and drips. He hated the indignity of having to ask to pee in a bottle held in place by the nurse. The sooner he could use his hands the better he thought.

Not long before lunch. Harpal Shaik arrived carrying a container covered with tin foil.

"Don't tell me you've come to take a sample too!" joked Bruce who was feeling the benefit of having slept a little.

"No, said Harpal, "it's a present from my mother. Both my parents and the

Called into Question

wider family send their best wishes. Mama made you some kheer to help you regain your strength! She remembered how much you liked it when you came to ours."

Bruce laughed. "That's kind of her. What is it with these mums who are desperate to feed us when there is a problem? My mum wanted to bring in pasta!"

"My mother is desperate to feed me full stop. She does not need a crisis by way of excuse. But I guess it's a primitive instinct to nourish, a way of perpetuating the breast-feeding reflex."

"I hope that wasn't what your mother was thinking of when she made this for me!"

Harpal laughed. "No, perhaps not. Anyway, moving on, how are you? You look a lot better than when I saw you loaded into the ambulance. Had me worried, I can tell you."

"Harpal I don't really know what happened. Grab that chair. I need you to fill in the gaps for me."

Harpal sat down beside the bed.

"First, I want to say thank you. The doctor told me what I good job you'd done. Saved my life apparently."

"I'm not sure about that. I think they're being over-dramatic."

"And I think you are being over-modest. The bullet clipped an artery. I could have bled to death there and then. I owe you. When did you get so good at First Aid?"

"It was common sense really. I could see you were bleeding. When we were at Eynsham Hall, I enjoyed the First Aid module. Inspired me to find out more so I took a book out of the library. *"What to do in an accident."*

"Glad you did. Perhaps you should have been a doctor." said Bruce.

Harpal hesitated a moment. "Perhaps I should have, perhaps I should. My folks would love that."

"Anyway, what's the news about the raid? My head was scrambled when I first came round. Now I'm not sure what really happened and what I am imagining. I think I remember the car crashing and then chasing the guy who jumped out of the car."

"Ok, I'll pick it up from there." said Harpal. "Then I'll pass on what I've heard since from some of the others about what had happened at the house before. When the car crashed I saw that little guy, who by the way is Pete Brady himself, the main man, run out of the tunnel and saw you start to chase him. I was more concerned about whether the driver was going to emerge. I looked in through the open passenger door. The driver was unconscious but breathing. He had a head wound. You scored a bulls-eye with that brick. The first car with our guys arrived at that point. Two of them said they'd deal with the driver. I told the others where I'd seen you head off. The handler let his dog go and we started chasing. Hearing another shot was terrible. I was ahead of the others and got to you first. There was no way that dog was going to let Brady go."

"You were out of it. Lying on him. For a moment, I feared the worst. I rolled you over and saw the wound in your tunic. Blood was pulsing out. I knew I had to get as much pressure to your chest and shoulder as possible. I was pretty much kneeling on you and using my weight to staunch it. Brady was nicked and hand-cuffed. Three of the guys picked you up while I applied as much pressure as I could. Nightmare scrambling back to the lane. Fortunately, the ambulance got there almost as soon as we lay you down on a groundsheet near the bridge. They were brilliant and obviously dealt with you before the injured driver."

"Should think so too." interrupted Bruce.

"So that was it basically. We all went back to the nick and apart from those who weren't tied up with charging people had a de-brief."

"So, what happened at the house?"

"Coming to that. Patience."

"I am being a patient and I don't like it."

"Apparently when they stormed the house, there were two guys dozing just inside the door. Probably meant to be on look-out. A couple of whisky bottles suggested they had got distracted. Brady and the driver came down the backstairs when they heard the commotion. Our guys followed, those two shots we heard were fired as they got into the car. No-one was hit. That's when they came belting our way. The rest as they say is history and you know it."

"So where are the four men now? asked Bruce.

"The driver is here in the hospital. He's under observation, medical and custodial. That's also one of the reasons there is a guard outside your room. Standard procedure apparently. Brady and the two sleeping beauties are in the cells at our nick. I know Brady's been charged with attempted murder for starters. Don't know what they'll do the other two for at this stage."

"Guess it depends what else they've been involved with." said Bruce who was grateful to have a fuller picture of the drama in which he had played a starring role.

"The local and national news carried reports this morning. Not much detail; four men are in police custody following a raid by detectives from Thames Valley Police. It is believed the men are allegedly involved in organized crime. A uniform officer who was shot in the raid is in a stable condition in hospital. No names, no locations."

"Did Collins say anything?" Bruce asked.

"Not much to the team but he caught me as I was leaving. He was glowing with pleasure, but he said to say to you when I saw you bad luck about being shot."

"Ha! As simple as that eh?" Bruce snorted. "He was so sure they were unarmed. So much for good intelligence."

"I am sure he'll be happy to have that discussion with you at some point. You may want to wait till you are out of hospital. On second thoughts, it might be a smart move to be in hospital already when you question the great man's professional judgement!"

Chapter 27

Bruce was dozing after lunch when he had an unexpected but not unwelcome visitor.

"What are you doing here? I didn't expect to see you."

"I thought I would come and see the hero before he becomes famous and I have to pay for the privilege. I mean why pay for something you when you can have it for free?"

Apart from one brief glimpse of her in jeans Bruce had only seen Holly in either her work clothes or in sports kit. Standing just inside the door of his room she looked like he expected a girl from her home background to look. She was wearing her tight-fitting loon jeans, blue suede desert boots and a white Indian cotton top with a scoop neck-line. She had a necklace made from love-beads and matching bracelet. A patchwork bag in chambray blue was slung over one shoulder.

"You look smart. Is this your student look?"

"Something like that. It's my hospital visiting outfit actually." she said smiling at Bruce.
He smiled back and could not help thinking how fresh Holly looked. So often when she was working in an evening she had looked world weary and older than her years. Not surprising really. He wished he could understand how she

rationalized and coped with what she did.

"It's great to see you, thanks for coming. How on earth did you discover where I was? Harpal told me they have been keeping that quiet, for various reasons, probably unnecessarily."

Holly faltered a moment as she went to answer. "Um, I overheard one of the guys on patrol tell the paper man."

"The one by the station again? He does seem to be the fount of all knowledge. Perhaps I should start buying a daily paper from him when I get back to work. Or rather, if I go back to work."

"How are you feeling? Is it very painful?" asked Holly moving the conversation on.

"They seem to be controlling the pain quite well most of the time. Apparently, the surgeon is an expert in treating bullet wounds. Spent time in Northern Ireland. I've been told more than once how lucky I am."
"It does sound as though it could have been a lot worse. Were you frightened?" asked Holly sitting down bedside the bed.

"To be honest it all happened so fast I didn't really get a chance to think at the time."

"Instinctive heroism, something you were born to."

Bruce looked at Holly carefully to see if she was teasing him. He didn't think she was.

"I don't think it is fair to call it heroism. Like when people dive into icy rivers to rescue people or risk going into a burning building. You don't think, you just act. Last night I think that adrenalin and fear played a part in driving me on. I wanted to tackle Brady before he could turn on me. Oh, I shouldn't have said his name. Pretend you didn't hear that."

"Don't worry I won't tell anyone it was Pete Brady. Here I brought you a box of Maltesers."

Bruce was quiet for a moment. "That's kind. Put them in my drawer or my sisters will snaffle them."

Holly sat down again. "The other day you said you had a question you wanted to ask but it wasn't the right time. Is this as good a time as any? You're not racing anywhere are you?"

"I suppose so. It's probably nothing really but it's been on my mind for a while."

"Go on Bruce I can't bear the suspense. Better out than in!" she said with a mischievous smile.

Something in Bruce still made him hesitate. Perhaps he had misheard his mother. Also, if his worse fears were confirmed why was it an issue? Why

Called into Question 203

should it matter to him who his ex-fiancée went out with or became attached to?

"Ok. This may sound stupid or irrational, but I have an awful feeling that my ex-girlfriend Jenny might be going out with your ex Tom!" even as he heard himself speaking he realized how far-fetched his words must sound.

"Wow, Bruce. That is a surprise! Seriously?" Little seemed to faze Holly, but he could see that this had taken her by surprise.

"That would be weird. I know they say it's a small world but that would be something." Instinctively she had put her hand up to her mouth and was biting the side of her thumb nail. "What on earth makes you think that?"

"Something my mum told me. A few weeks ago, when she was out shopping she bumped into Jenny's mother. They had a bit of a chat. Mum asked after Jenny as she naturally would. Apparently, she is going out with a junior doctor from Surrey called Tom. I thought she must have started a new relationship because despite what she'd said about keeping in touch, she hasn't."

"I'm sorry about that Bruce, but I don't think it's my Tom, well obviously not *my* Tom, you know what I mean."

"You don't have to explain what that feels like. I catch myself still thinking of Jenny as *mine,* though while we were together I tried not to be possessive."

"Bruce, there must be hundreds, thousands even of nurse and doctors in London. The chances of it being our ex-es. No, it can't be."

"That's what I have told myself, over and over but the idea doesn't go away."

Holly sat looking up at the bag of saline fluid, dripping into the tube attached to Bruce's arm. Suddenly she seemed transfixed by it. Bruce watched her. He could tell she was thinking hard. When she was ready, in her own time she looked back at Bruce.

"Let's assume or pretend for a moment that what you've said is correct. In this seemingly random world two people, who have played a key role in the lives of each of us, have met each other. Who knows, they may even have fallen in love." Holly was speaking quickly, the words tumbling out like coins spilling on to the floor from a purse. "Does it matter? And if it does matter why does it matter?"

Bruce hesitated. He wanted to check that she had finished. Having played the scenario over and over in his head many times in recent weeks he had imagined what Holly's response would be. He had expected a gasp of shock, possibly tears. In the event this response had surprised him. Did she really think it did not matter, was of no consequence?

"Holly of course it matters. Can't you see? Because we know each other. Because I think…"

Bruce's parents arrived back for afternoon visiting. "Knock, knock! Can we come in?" said his mother brightly, putting her head round the door and stepping in simultaneously. Bruce stopped abruptly.

"Oh, you've got company. Sorry. No-one said." Sophia Hammond was assessing Holly even as she spoke in the way that only a mother can when she thinks she is meeting her son's girlfriend for the first time.

"We can come back in a bit if you'd like." Bruce's father was a master when it came to tact and politeness.

His wife evidently thought this was not a good idea. Turning to her son Sophia said, "Well are you going to introduce us?"

"Of course, mum, dad, this is Holly." Muir Hammond, lowered his head in greeting. Sophia smiled and offered her hand to Holly. "Holly, my parents, Muir and Sophia."

Bruce felt he was blushing with embarrassment and yet Holly looked unflustered, completely at ease.

"Do you work together? asked Bruce's father innocently, "or are you just friends?"

Bruce could see that his mother was in a state of high alert, listening for his answer, like a sheep dog waiting for its master's whistle.

"Holly and I met through work!" As he said this Bruce recognized that he needed to choose his words very carefully. "She's from Surrey and has been to Art College."

"How interesting." said Muir, who was always keen to meet and encourage young people who shared his passion for art.

His mother however clearly needed more information to go on to help her form an opinion of this newcomer in her son's life. "What are you doing work wise now?"

"I'm a waitress, just while I work out my next move."

"Oh, well you know what they say." Bruce wondered which of his collection of sayings his father would pull out on this occasion. "A spot of time in almost any form of customer service stands you in good stead for so many other positions in life. Good to learn that while you may be able to please all of the people some of the time you can't please all of the people all of the time."

Bruce looked away to avoid catching Holly's eye.

"Oh, that's so true Mr. Hammond." said Holly without hesitation. "Well, I ought to be off now. Glad to see you're ok Bruce. Hope to see you soon once you're out and about." She smiled and gave one of her trademark waves.

Bruce lay back on his pillow and looked at the ceiling. He closed his eyes and

Called into Question

braced himself for the imminent interrogation.

Holly had made a good impression on Bruce's father. "What a charming girl? Where did you say you met her?"

Bruce was spared from answering that tricky question by his mother's ambivalence. "Well, I am not surprised you fell for her Muir Hammond, an easy smile and a pair of tight-fitting jeans always did work for you, didn't they? Like father like son. But I am not so sure. I have my doubts. I can't quite put my finger on it, something not quite right. Little bit too sure with her answers."

"And who asked you anyway mum? You can't do a character assessment, or assassination more like, based on a few minutes of conversation."

"No need to jump down my throat. I can see you're feeling better. I have not assassinated her character. I am simply saying there's much more going on there than she was letting on."

"Mum, you've only just met her for goodness sake." Despite his protest Bruce wondered if all mothers were equipped with an emotional radar system to match his mother's.

"Whereas you clearly met her some time ago. Odd you haven't mentioned her." Sophia felt affronted by her son's apparent secrecy.

"She is just a friend, no more than that. And what is more I don't know how or why she came to visit. I don't even know where she lives!"

"That old line – she's just a friend. I really do not know why you men ever come out with such rubbish. She is visiting you in hospital outside of visiting hours. We are your parents and yet we had to get permission to see you. Either you have told the hospital she is your girlfriend or little madam there knows the right people."

"I promise you. She is not my girlfriend. I don't even know if she likes me."

Muir Hammond laughed. "I was just about to stand up for you and then you come out with priceless idiocy like that. Of course, she likes you. Even an alleged slow learner in the romance stakes like me can see it, Bruce. She has made it her business to track you down and to come and visit you. I would say she's keen."

Sophia looked triumphant. Bruce realized there was nothing to be gained by continuing the conversation. Ending it spared him explaining much that would be awkward.

"Harpal Shaik came in to see me earlier. The doctor told me he saved my life."

"He must come to tea one Sunday. Perhaps while you are convalescing. We would love to meet him properly. Not least to say thank you."
"Good idea, Dad, I think he'd like that."

Chapter 28

July 4th

Crazy time. B has been shot. Thank God he is going to be ok. Sounds like his friend saved his life. I visited him in hospital. He was very emotional – not surprisingly. He has got a mad idea that our exes have got together. Very worked up about it. Seemed he was about to say something important when his parents arrived. Like his dad but don't think his mum liked me. Left note with nurse – bit silly.
Saw A-M in town. She seems very down – wouldn't say why.

Chapter 29

"Well good morning. How are you feeling? It makes a change to have to wake a patient." Fiona opened the blinds in Bruce's room. He blinked as shafts of early morning light streamed in. Outside in the main ward Bruce could hear Fiona's colleagues cajoling patients in to the busy routine of a new day.

"Looks as though your body decided it needed to do some catching up on the sleep front after all the action of the last few days. How's your shoulder feeling? I will change the dressing once I've checked your temperature and blood pressure."

"Thanks. It's quite sore and stiff but you're right, I did sleep well."

Fiona popped a thermometer into Bruce's mouth. "Keep that under your tongue while I take your blood pressure. The doctor hopes to take at least one of these IV lines out today. You'll feel more comfortable."

Bruce nodded and hummed his approval being careful not to break the thermometer.

"I've got something for you," she said with a broad smile, "your lady friend asked me to give you this." She reached into her pocket and took out a plain white postcard, folded in half and addressed to "PC B Hammond".

"I gather she disappeared sharpish when your folks arrived. I saw her sitting outside in the corridor writing when I went to empty some pans in the sluice. How long have you been going out?" She extracted the thermometer from Bruce's mouth just in time for him to reply.

"We are not going out. We are just friends." He struggled to hide his exasperation.

"Good friends?" asked Fiona winking.

"No, just friends."

"Ok I get the message. Run along nosey nurse I am desperate to read this note from my *I swear she's only a friend*." She swept out closing the door as she went.

Bruce unfolded the card. Holly's handwriting was neat and girly in style with extravagant loops and swirls. She had a habit of underlining words for emphasis.

Bruce, thought it best to disappear. That was <u>embarrassing</u>. Hope I did ok and it wasn't <u>too</u> difficult for you. I <u>really</u> would like to come to your home one day. I was going to give you my phone number (Cheston 4177). It's a payphone in the hallway of my flats. Suggest you give three rings, ring off then give another three and I'll know it's you. <u>Want to know what you were going to say</u>. Get well soon. Hollyx
PS your dad is nice.

Bruce read the note three times. The forensics department would have been impressed with the way he examined it. He sniffed it in the hope of smelling a hint of her perfume. He tried to hear Holly's voice as he read it. He thought the extravagant script matched the expressive gestures she used when speaking. The way she had signed off was typical of one of her casual departing waves. Eventually he folded it over and tucked it underneath his wash bag in the bedside unit.

He was thrilled to have a contact number. He would ring her as soon as he was out of hospital. She had said she wanted to see him once he was up and about. He looked forward to re-arranging a visit on a Sunday afternoon when he would have the house to himself.

After breakfast one of the nursing auxiliaries knocked on his door. "Nurse Fiona wants me to give you a shave if you'd like one. Sounds like they're going to let one or two photographers see you later. She says you'll want to look your best."

"You know more than me." replied Bruce. "I'll be glad when I can do this for myself, thank you."

"That's alright," replied the auxiliary, a plain but happy-looking woman in her forties. "It's my job. You'll be able to manage once they've taken your drips out. Perhaps tomorrow."

Bruce leaned back against the pillows, closed his eyes and tried to relax as best he could. Being washed and shaved by someone else was not something he enjoyed. It seemed an invasion of his privacy and underlined his temporary state of dependence. He recognized that he liked to feel in control of his life and destiny. He wondered if the morning ablutions would be more pleasurable if they were done by one of the younger attractive nurses. He quickly tried to dismiss this thought to avoid the embarrassment of giving the auxiliary the wrong idea. He was not entirely successful.

He turned his mind to the prospect of having to face reporters and photographers. He was conscious too of having to resolve the questions about his future which had of necessity been put on the back-burner over the last few days. A period of convalescence would give him time and space to think.

Fiona popped her head round the door. Bruce was covered in shaving foam. "An Inspector Middleton just rang. He's coming in to see you – will be here in twenty minutes. Bruce raised his left hand in acknowledgement. His nurse specialized in catching him when he could not speak. Perhaps it was a trick of the trade, developed by busy people as a self-preservation tactic.

Bruce had been impressed by Bob Middleton ever since their first encounter outside the night club at New Year. He was one of those rare men who managed to more than justify the high opinion many had of him. He accomplished this by acting in an understated way. Bruce had benefited from his fairness and wisdom. He realized now that Middleton was not afraid to confront DCI Ted Collins despite being inferior in rank to the bullying detective. Bruce felt embarrassed when he reflected on his early exchanges with him.

Fiona showed the Inspector into the room. "I hope he's behaving himself nurse and doing what you tell him."

"He's not bad actually. We know how to handle young men in uniform. They bring the squaddies from Windsor Barracks here. They keep us on our toes, I can tell you."

"I bet they do," laughed Middleton, "Well let me know if this one gives you any trouble."

Fiona left the men to talk, closing the door behind her.

"And I hope they are looking after you well, PC Hammond."

"Yes, they are, thank you sir."

"Well, it's good to know you are on the mend. We thought we should give the press the chance to see you before you look too healthy. Are you ok with having some photos taken? It will, I am afraid, give you a degree of fame or notoriety. Nothing you won't be able to handle, I'm sure."

"Do I have a choice, sir?"

"Not really, Bruce. A police officer being shot on duty is still big news. We should probably be glad it is. It also is good PR for us and for the police service generally. Given how little respect there is around these days the view from above is that we should capitalize on opportunities like this."

"I understand, sir."

"I do need to point out a couple of things. Sorry if they seem obvious to you. Try not to look too healthy and chirpy for the cameras. Hang dog expression the order of the day. Think of the Clement Freud dog food ad; Henry's not been getting his Minced Morsels etcetera."

"I don't think I can manage an impression, but I get the idea."

"Talking of Minced Morsels, what's the food like in here?"

"Not bad, sir." said Bruce. "To be honest I've not felt like much up to now. We're not talking Michelin stars, but I imagine it's better than they serve in Wandsworth or the Scrubs."

"I hope so. Not much of a recommendation I must say. While we're on the subject I hope you don't feel too imprisoned, having a guard outside. Pete Brady is a serious gangster and has connections to some very unpleasant characters. We thought we ought to be on the safe side."

"I haven't been outside the room yet so have been unaware of it really."

"Good." Inspector Middleton went on to impress on Bruce the importance when talking to journalists of not saying anything that could prejudice the outcome of the ensuing trial. He could talk about how he felt and answer questions about his background if he wanted to. The stock answer to any requests for detail about the incident was to say it was *sub judice*.

"I know you, more than most, will be aware of how important that is. I am sorry you are going to have two big trials hanging over you, what with this and the accident. They will form a big part of life over the next year or so."

"I have to admit, that had begun to dawn on me. I can't pretend I'll be looking forward to them. I can't quite imagine what I'll be doing by then."

"So, you're still thinking of calling it a day, are you?"

"To be honest I'm not really sure what I'm thinking. I've been rather all over the place lately."

"Not surprising in the light of all that's gone on. I hope you'll take your time. In terms of your injury you will probably get an award from Criminal Injuries Compensation Board. It won't take the pain away now but in the longer run it might be a nice sweetener for what's been an awful experience. Oh, I know what else I was going to tell you. Something that happened last night which I thought would interest and amuse you."

"What's that then?"

"Burglary on the Firs estate. We got a call first thing. People had woken up and discovered they had been broken into although that's not really the right term. At some point in the night, someone had taken out the putty around a downstairs window and carefully removed the whole pane of glass. They propped it against the wall outside, clambered in and helped themselves to one or two valuables and some small electrical goods."

"Cool customer with a steady hand." remarked Bruce.

"Hang on. I'm not finished yet. There's more and it gets better. The house in question is a semi-detached like most on the estate. The neighbours woke up when they heard the Panda car arrive at just gone six. They went downstairs and discovered the same thing had happened to them. The cheeky blighters did one and then popped next door and went through the whole process again. The second family usually live in chaos, but the intruder had left the books and clobber on the window sill neatly stacked!"

"Seriously?"

The inspector nodded.

"You almost have to admire their nerve, don't you?" said Bruce.

"That's my point, Bruce. To succeed in lots of settings in life you must be patient, take your time and hold your nerve. Anyway, I'll be getting on and leave you to the tender mercies of the press hounds. There should be a press officer from HQ arriving soon. So, you won't be on your own."

"Goodbye sir. Thanks for the visit and the advice."

Chapter 30

Bruce was released from hospital after ten days. His surgeon Mr. Gannon signed him off work for a month. He warned him that if he neglected his regime of physio exercises it would be considerably longer before he could return to full duties. Bruce assured him he was used to being disciplined about exercise and would look forward to being able to be active again. Although he would feel discomfort for some while there would be no lasting damage in the long term. "Obviously you will have the two scars by way of life-long mementoes of the shooting. By the time you have children they will be badges of honour, and if you have grand-children they will be the trigger of any number of tall stories." said the surgeon with a warm smile.

"Thank you for all you have done for me, doctor. I really appreciate it."

"Please, I was just doing my job as you were doing yours. I can't over-emphasize what a lucky young man you are. With you and your assailant both falling to the ground the shot could have gone anywhere. From such close range, you really are fortunate to be alive. Somebody up there was looking after you. I hope you'll make the most of your reprieve."

Bruce had not expected a lesson in life from the medic. As he mulled over the doctor's words he realized that he shouldn't be so surprised. To get to the top of that profession, as Dr. Gannon clearly had, must have taken a lot of hard work over a prolonged period. To keep at it must require determination and probably a strong sense of calling or inner motivation. He envied anyone with such a conviction.

Bruce was unable to drive until the mobility had returned to his shoulder. Being dependent on lifts from his parents or friends was irksome. Consequently, being confined to the house soon became a source of frustration. There was at least the compensation of being able to watch and to listen to coverage of the England v Australia test matches. England had been crushed in the first game of the series and were no match for the fast bowling pair of Lillee and Thomson. Bruce was not impressed with the selectors' decision to bring in a grey-haired bespectacled batsman in the form of David Steele instead of a more dashing younger man.

Bruce did not confide in anyone about his note from Holly. He kept it tucked in his passport in his bedside drawer, underneath his warrant card. The card had a grainy photo of Bruce, taken in his first week at the Thames Valley Police Headquarters near Oxford. Those early days seemed an age away despite being less than a year before. So much had happened, so much had changed. At the back of the drawer was the picture of Jenny he had carried in his wallet. There was also a packet of Durex condoms, with only one missing. He had felt tempted to throw them away. Each time he saw them was a painful reminder. It was as though the opened packet was mocking him. He left them where they were for the time being.

Although he read over the card from Holly on at least a daily basis and found himself replaying their last conversation in his head repeatedly, Bruce had not rung her. Initially he told himself that it would be better to wait until he was stronger. Also, his mother had insisted that they postpone their next scheduled weekend away at least for a fortnight so that she could nurse Bruce. When they eventually fixed their next break, Bruce was feeling much stronger and was going out for short walks and even in to town on a bus. However, he still felt hesitant about ringing. He was unsure about what was holding him back. Shyness with girls had not been an issue previously.

He disliked himself intensely on those rare occasions in life when he was indecisive. Eventually his parents announced that they had rearranged their weekend break. His resolve strengthened with a couple of glasses of rum and coke he picked up the phone one afternoon when he was home alone. He let it ring three times twice and then rang again as per Holly's instructions. He was relieved to hear her answer, albeit non-commitally.
"Holly, it's Bruce."

"Hello. I thought you'd got cold feet. How are you doing?"

"I'm fine thanks. I'm sorry I haven't got around to ringing you before now. It's just never quite seemed like the right time."

"That's alright. It went through my mind that perhaps the nurse hadn't passed on my note or that it had been intercepted by your mother."

Bruce laughed. "No, she didn't get her hands on it fortunately."

"Your mum didn't like me, did she?"

Bruce hesitated. "I thought not." said Holly.

"Er, no, um, it's just she doesn't like surprises." Bruce knew he sounded unconvincing.

"It's okay Bruce, you don't have to pretend. It wasn't hard to pick up the vibes coming my way from her."

"Don't take it too personally Holly, you know what they say about Italian mothers, no girl will ever be good enough for their precious sons."
"I think that might be mothers the world over." laughed Holly. "Anyway, it's good to hear you."

"It's good to hear you too. I am ringing because my parents are going away the last weekend of the month. I wondered how you'd feel about coming over one afternoon like we'd discussed." Bruce was relieved to have finally got the words out. "I quite understand if you don't."

"Bruce, I'd like to. That would be nice, and I trust you. Tea at the Manse sounds grand."

Bruce suspected Holly was teasing him but nevertheless said "Great! Come on the Sunday afternoon about half two."

"Okeydokey, see you then. Thanks."

Bruce decided that he would not mention anything to his parents about his arrangement with Holly. He was pleasantly surprised to discover that the element of secrecy heightened his sense of anticipation and excitement. One evening lying on his bed thinking about how the afternoon might unfold he opened his bedside drawer and checked the packet of Durex were still there. He caught himself and felt disappointed. He genuinely did not want to take advantage of the situation with Holly. He remembered how hesitant she had looked the first evening they had met. He recalled too the night she had been upset and allowed him to comfort her. Knowing all she had been through he thought he owed it to her to keep things purely platonic. However, he also found himself revisiting those occasions when he thought she was flirting with him or giving positive signals. As in so many areas of his life he realized that he was seriously conflicted.

He wished his parents had not interrupted him when he was in hospital. He had hoped that Holly would have guessed what he had been about to say. It puzzled him as to how she could be so relaxed about the idea of Tom and Jenny possibly having got together. In his mind that was a massive obstacle to any chance of a relationship with Holly.

The act of fixing a date for Holly to come and visit energized Bruce. He extended the range of his morning walks; along the Thames and out across Windsor Great Park marveling at the giant oaks which, to his mind, resembled monsters from an animated cartoon film. He realized in retrospect that he had been in shock, as he had been warned he would be, and that this shock had produced a numb inertia in him. As the weekend grew closer he took pleasure in planning how to entertain Holly. He wanted her to feel that he had made an effort. He wanted her to feel special. His initial erotic fantasies were under control. He was confident that he would be able to make her feel relaxed and appreciated as a friend and not desired as a sex object. He was beginning to envisage alternative future scenarios for himself and wanted Holly to be able to do the same. Perhaps if this proved possible, then there might be a chance further down the line when, free of the ugliness of Cheston, they might be able to explore something more than friendship.

Bruce toyed with the idea of telling Harpal about his date with Holly. The disappointment Bruce had felt when hearing about Harpal's engagement was not something he wanted to inflict on his friend. He knew that Harpal had wanted Bruce to recognize and own his feelings for Holly. He imagined his friend would be pleased with this turn of events. Eventually, he decided it might be wiser not to run ahead of himself. If the afternoon went well, he would confide in his friend at the earliest opportunity. Being off work and unable to drive had meant the two men had seen less of each other. Bruce sensed that in recent weeks Harpal had become more preoccupied with plans for his own future.

Bruce could not imagine what his mother would make of his relationship with Holly, especially if she ever discovered the facts about her life to date. On the Thursday before the family was due to go away Sophia Hammond unwittingly removed a major obstacle to her son developing a romantic attachment to Holly. She had been into Windsor to buy some "bits and pieces" for the weekend away. Hearing her return Bruce thought he would show willing and offered to make a cup of tea. They sat together at the kitchen table while the pot was brewing.

"Did you have a good time?" asked Bruce grateful for the chance of conversation after a day on his own.

"Yes, I did thanks. I got everything I wanted and something for Hannah's birthday next month."

"Did you meet any of your friends, anyone you know?"

"Well I did see Rose again, but I know you won't want to hear about that." Sophia Hammond reached for the tea pot and began to pour.

"It's okay, that was just bad timing before. I am sorry. It feels like a lifetime ago. So, what's the news?"

"Are you sure you want to know?" Sophia Hammond, looked at her son's face nervously. She had struggled with feeling estranged from her son and did not want to jeopardize their recent rapprochement.

Bruce stirred his tea. "Sure."

"Well, Jenny and this doctor are still going out together. Her mum and dad have met him now. Apparently, Tim seems like a nice young man."
Bruce was about to sip his tea. He stopped as though in suspended animation. His mother was taken aback. "Are you alright, darling?"

"Say what you just said again. The last bit."

"I think I said; *apparently Tim seems like a nice young man.* Why? What's the matter?"

"Bear with me, Mum. This is important. What is this doctor guy's name?"

"It's Tim. I still don't know why it is important." Bruce's mother was looking at her son intently, worried that he might have overdone things through the day.

"It just is. You are sure his name is Tim. It's just that when you told me about Jenny's new boyfriend originally you said he was called Tom."

"Did I? I am sorry I must have misheard. You know what I am like with names. I don't see why it's a big deal."

"You are absolutely sure you've got it right now."

"Yes, Bruce, I am, and I'll tell you why. Jenny's mum says he has quite a posh name, double-barreled Brooke-Jarvis. She said they have joked about him sounding like that funny man in the Goodies, Tim Brooke something or other."

"Taylor. Tim Brooke Taylor mum. You really are useless with names, aren't you?" Bruce was smiling as he said this, digesting this unexpected piece of news.

Called into Question

"Aren't you going to tell me why this is so important to you? You worry me Bruce."

"I know Mum, I'm sorry. I don't mean to. I can't tell you now, but I expect I will one day."

Bruce went up to his room. He picked out Crosby, Stills, Nash and Young's album *"So Far"*, put it on the turntable and lay back on his bed. He felt happier than he'd felt for a long time. The sense of relief was enormous. He realized how much he had allowed the unlikely scenario to dominate his thoughts.

The band broke into the second track *"Hopelessly Hoping"*. Bruce smiled to himself, got up, turned up the volume and opened his bedroom window wide.

Chapter 31

July 31st

Bad week. Strangely quiet. Going to B's for tea – rhymes! Decided to take the bus and walk. Haven't decided what to wear. Think he likes the student look. Nothing too sexy – think he's alright but feel torn myself. Weird – I know I should tell him about stuff and my plan, but not sure this is right time.

Chapter 32

This is a mistake. What am I doing? Why have I invited a prostitute to tea? Tea – it's what my parents do for old ladies! Bruce woke on the long-awaited Sunday morning in the grip of doubt. He had gone to bed the night before in a state of euphoric excitement but now the day had dawned that had evaporated. He wondered not for the first time if Holly was humouring him. Yet she had seemed genuinely pleased to be invited. Bruce did not think he had misread her completely. He did recognize however that his ability to understand people and situations was not quite as sharp as it had been. Briefly he entertained the idea of ringing Holly and making an excuse for cancelling their arrangement. He quickly dismissed this thought and decided to throw himself into preparations.

He had enjoyed buying what he thought he needed to lay on a good spread. Surveying it on the kitchen table he realized he had bought enough to feed a Sunday school tea-party. He hoped Holly would be hungry otherwise disposing of the leftovers would be a challenge. He did not want to leave evidence of his entertaining for his mother to discover on her return.

Bruce was by nature an optimist who liked to have a Plan B in place. He knew that this trait was inherited as an expression of his mother's romanticism tempered by his father's realism. He hoped the weather would be fine so that they could eat on the back lawn, maybe even lie on the sun-loungers. If the meteorological gods conspired against him, they could base themselves in the front room with the two large cream sofas. In the event the day was fine,

August had put on her Sunday best for the occasion!

Half an hour before Holly was due Bruce, having laid out the tea and boiled the kettle, went upstairs to change. He had not been this nervous since his first date with Jenny. On that occasion, he had cut himself shaving and had set off with a small piece of cotton wall on his chin which he had meant to take off at the last moment.

His best Levi's were washed and ready. He pulled on a skin-tight yellow grandad vest, tied his Green Flash tennis shoes and stood in front of the full-length mirror in his room. Standing with his thumbs hitched in his belt he looked as though he were posing for a clothing catalogue or for Jackie magazine. He smiled at the thought and was glad Hannah and Sarah were not around to tease him or to ask awkward questions.

He had toyed with the idea of bringing his record deck downstairs but decided that might look as if he were trying too hard. He was over-thinking things and told himself to relax. Easier said than done.

Holly arrived slightly early which pleased Bruce. He hated lateness in himself and in others.

"Hi Bruce. Sorry I'm a bit early. It's just the way the bus times worked out. I walked from the end of the road. There are some seriously smart places in this village aren't there. This is nice. Big." Holly was nervous and even more chatty than normal.

Called into Question

"It is but obviously we don't own it. Dad is always apologizing for it, I suppose a bit like I am now. He describes it as a glorified council house. They can't do anything to it without getting permission from a committee. I think that's why they enjoy having their own little place in the Cotswolds. They bought it with an inheritance and like being able to do exactly what they want with it. Come on through to the kitchen. The kettle has boiled."

"Ooh do you mind if I explore in here while you make the tea? I am ever so nosey really. It will give me more of an idea about your family."

"Be my guest, which of course you are." said Bruce laughing. He watched Holly go into the front room. She looked great in her jeans, no wonder she had figured on Harpal's radar at the sports centre. She was wearing a tie-dye purple and white t-shirt and leather thong hippy sandals. "Enjoying the view?" she said suddenly without turning around.

Bruce laughed. "Guilty as charged."

"Go and make that tea while I enjoy snooping."

Bruce went along to the kitchen. He made the tea and while it brewed he took a plate of assorted sandwiches and a plate of cake, Battenberg and Victoria sponge, out into the garden. He went back into the house and stood quietly at the lounge door to watching Holly as she picked up various photo frames and studied them carefully.

"If you are very good I'll show you the family photo albums."

Holly jumped and turned to look at Bruce. She had a framed family group in her hand. It was taken by the local paper when Bruce's father had taken up his post. "You startled me." she said. Bruce could see that she had tears in her eyes.

"Bruce, do you believe people can really make new starts? I look at these pictures of your family and I can't see how that's ever going to be my life. Not from where I am now." Holly wiped her eyes. "Sorry, ignore me."

Bruce was taken aback by how quickly the conversation had turned in a direction that he hoped it might go with some careful and gentle prompting. He wondered if he should comfort her, but a second instinct told him to hold back.

"I'd like to think people can make new starts but I'm not sure. I'm not sure of very much right now. When I was growing up, I must have been about ten, we had a young woman come and live with us for a few months. I just accepted it as part of dad's work at the time. Later I learned she was the daughter of another minister from elsewhere in the country. She'd had a baby but had given it up for adoption. I guess she came to us to get some space away from her life. I remember she came to church with us. She went on to become a youth worker and now manages a big outward bound centre for the Methodist church. She's married I think. So, you see, we were brought up believing in the importance of forgiveness and fresh starts. My dad loves quoting a Bible verse about people becoming a new person and leaving the old stuff behind, so they can live a new life. As verses go it's one of his better ones."

Bruce looked across at Holly. She had tears rolling down her cheeks. He remembered to his horror Holly's experience of getting pregnant and having an abortion. How could he be so insensitive?

"Holly I'm sorry I didn't think. Stupid of me." He moved towards her.

She put her hand up to stop him. "It's okay Bruce. It's sad, but in a strange way that's good to hear. I'm glad that girl had a choice. Your folks are good people, aren't they? Explains why you're a good guy."

"I don't feel a very good guy, these days."

Holly had recovered her poise. "I know you don't, but you are. I know a fair bit about men and trust me you are one of the better ones. Now where's this tea you threatened me with?"

Bruce could see she wanted to move on.

"Ok. Come out into the garden. I've put the stuff out there."

Bruce collected a tray with the tea pot and cups from the kitchen and led Holly out into the garden.

"Bruce this is amazing. There's so much. Who else have you invited?"

"No-one. I think I did get rather carried away."

"I'll need to be carried away if I eat all that. Are you fattening me up for market? It is really kind."

They settled on the sun loungers either side of a white wicker table which was straining under the weight of the food.

"It's a lovely garden. Who looks after it?"

"I often cut the grass but really it's mum's department. She loves it. I think she tries to recreate a little bit of Italy here. Even though she grew up here in England there is part of her, I think, that has always craved the sunshine and Mediterranean lifestyle."

"I can see that. The garden has that sort of feel. It's not classic English. It reminds me of the garden we had when I was growing up. My father had a taste for the exotic." She went quiet for a while.

"Do you often think back to those days? If, you don't mind me asking?" Bruce hoped he had not jumped in clumsily.

"No. I don't mind. To be honest I should probably think about those times more often than I do. Perhaps the memories would inspire me to do more."

"That's honest. Talking of memories good and bad, I've got something interesting to tell you. I learned that Jenny's new boyfriend is a Tim not a Tom! We can relax."

Holly laughed and lay back on the lounger. "I told you. Aren't you funny getting all worked up about it?"

"Mum misheard the first time. So that's a relief."

"Bruce, why is it a relief. I couldn't see why it was such a big deal, even if it had been Jenny and Tom, so what? The past is the past. We can't undo it."

"You don't get it? What I don't get is how *you* could be so relaxed about it. If our friendship is going to develop we would find it strange knowing our ex-es had got together." Bruce offered Holly the plate of sandwiches.

"No thanks. Bruce what do you mean by "*our friendship develop*"? We are friends, we work in the same area and we get on, but it can't ever be more than that."

"Holly, I should have said this before now. I nearly did. I was going to tell you when you came to see me in hospital, but my folks arrived. I really like you and have been wondering at some point down the line, when things have changed for us, if we might be more than friends." Bruce was afraid he was gabbling but was glad to have finally told Holly how he felt.

"Oh Bruce. You are such a romantic. Get real. You are a police officer. I work as a prostitute. It isn't going to happen. It can't happen. This is life, not some film or fairy story."

"But Holly, back in the house you said I was a good guy. It sounds like you like me. I've told you what I feel about you. Where's the problem? Why can't it work? We could make it work, if we wanted to. I don't think I am going to stay in the police and I don't care that you're a prostitute. You can change too."

Holly stood up. Her eyes were blazing. "You want to talk. Let's really talk. Bruce, you hardly know me. Let me tell you some stuff and then you can see if you still want to hold on to your dream. I'm used to being the subject of men's fantasies, but usually those fantasies involve them undressing me, tying me up, doing stuff you wouldn't want to hear about. And do you know I can cope in my own way with that, but your fantasy is different. Yours is of me being a loving wife, of kids and a dog and roses round the door. It isn't going to happen. That train left the station for me a long time ago. And something else Bruce. I am not a prostitute. I work *as* a prostitute. Big difference. I am still a person. Please remember that. It's how I cope. I am still a person, one who has to play a role I don't like."

Bruce stood up to face Holly. "I know you are. You see, you want to change. You want to be different. Let's help each other."

"There you go again, dreaming." Holly looked up at the sky in exasperation as though looking for inspiration. "Let me spell it out. Sit down!"

Bruce did as he was told. Holly sat down on the side of the lounger facing him.

"You must have wondered what I do and how I cope."

He nodded. He had his hands clasped between his knees looking down at the brown sun-scorched grass.

"Men come to me not just because they are frustrated and want sex in some form or another. Most of the ones who come to me want me to listen, to at least give the impression I'm interested in what they are saying. I'm an actress really Bruce. And sometimes I think I am a counselor. I play a role. You've seen me in my outfits when I am working. The heavy make-up and all that. That's my costume. When I go off to work, I tell myself I am going on stage. It helps me keep it separate, in my own mind at least." She paused.

Bruce looked up at her and met her eyes briefly. "I understand that, but how do you cope with the actual sex part. Making love goes beyond the physical, it's emotional; spiritual even if you like."

"There you go again. Bruce the romantic idealist. It can be those things and it's great when it is. I knew that briefly with Tom, but I assure you for lots of people, even married people it isn't. That's why men come to girls like me. I can't speak for others but for me, it's an act like I said. I pretend, I make the sounds, make them feel like they are good lovers and they go away and for a while at least they feel better about themselves."

Bruce was looking down at his feet again. "You must have boundaries Holly." "Oh, I do. Do you want me to spell them out? I stay in control and lay down the rules. If they don't like it, they can go elsewhere. Plenty of choice. I don't do anything that involves my mouth, not even kissing. I am what I suppose you would say good with my hands. Quite a few of my regulars don't even want, or can't even do, the so-called full sex thing but if they do it's always with a condom, no exceptions."

"You make it sound so matter of fact."

"That's because as a matter of fact it is a matter of fact. It's what I do. It's how I pay my bills. Now shall I go?"

Bruce took a deep breath and ran his hands through his hair as he exhaled. "No, please don't. I still feel the same. We could make a plan together, help each other to change."

"You think you could deal with that. You think my past wouldn't haunt you. I've got pregnant, I've had an abortion, run away from home and I have sex with men my father's age for money and you think you can deal with all that? That you can forgive that? I tell you I can't forgive myself for that, so I know you can't."

"How do you know if you don't let me try?"

"Bruce, only half an hour ago you admitted yourself you're not sure you believe in fresh starts. I think you want to. I also think you're not over Jenny. You're trying to get over her. You've convinced yourself you're in love with me but it's just a way subconsciously of trying to move on. Listen, if we were together there'd be times like all couples when we'd argue and that's when you'd throw my crappy dirty past in my face. I punish myself every day. I know you would too, and I couldn't blame you. It wouldn't work."

Bruce had been listening carefully. Now he looked at her and reached out and took her hands in his. "You can't know that for sure. We can't know unless we try."

Holly left her hands in his. She was looking down now. Tears began to stream. She was shaking her head as though arguing with herself. Bruce leaned forward and rested his forehead against hers. He let go out of her hands and cupped her face in them, wiping her tears away gently with his thumbs. He leaned forward and kissed both cheeks in turn. Holly closed her eyes. Bruce kissed her very lightly on the mouth, his bottom lip catching the edge of her top lip and lingering for a second or two. The moment was electric. He felt an involuntary shudder go through her body. Holly looked at Bruce with what he always would remember could only be described as wonderment in her eyes. He put one hand behind her head, leaned forward again and kissed her fully on the mouth. She responded, their tongues gently touching, exploring tentatively. Bruce stroked her hair with his fingers. Holly sighed gently as Bruce ended the kiss. He moved her hair back with his hand and bent in close inhaling her perfume as he kissed her neck.

Suddenly Holly pulled back from him. "Bruce, I am so sorry, so sorry. What am I doing?"

"I know you are, but you didn't wrong *me* with any of that stuff. You don't have to apologize to me. I know it's not what you want."

Holly let go of him. She stood up and moved three or four paces away from where they'd been sitting.

"This is wrong. I am sorry it can't happen."

"Holly don't start that again. I know you felt what I felt when we kissed. That was way beyond desire, more than being turned on."

"Bruce, please stop. I've got to tell you something. Something awful."

Bruce had stood up and was about to move towards her. "Awful, something more?"

Holly put her hand over her mouth and nodded, deeply distressed.

"Holly tell me, what is it?"

She looked at him. "I am so sorry. DCI Ted Collins is one of my regulars, my most regular. I am one of his network."

Bruce stopped in his tracks, completely stunned.

"I am so sorry. That's why we can't be. It can't happen." Holly stood and began to weep silently, uncontrollably.

The two of them stood as though frozen. Bruce could feel ringing in his ears, as though Holly's words had been spoken into a giant echo chamber. He felt hollow. Holly took some deep breaths. She walked slowly towards where Bruce still stood transfixed, his arms crossed close to his body, hugging himself.

She put one hand on his forearm. "Forgive me. I'll go. You stay here. I'll see myself out."

Her touch and voice broke the spell that appeared to have gripped him.

"How could you? I can't believe it. When you say you're one of his network, you mean one of his informers?"

Holly nodded without making eye contact.

"That makes sense of some stuff. How he knew about us and how you knew about me. Oh my God, you've played me, haven't you? You must think I'm a complete mug. I don't get it. Early on he slagged you off to me."

"Good word." Holly said bitterly. "Yes, he would have done. That's what he's like. He's cunning and sly. I'll just go like I said."

"No don't, you can't just walk away. You owe me that. That kiss, the kind words, all of that. What did it mean? How could you betray me like that?" Bruce was walking back and forward, going around in circles in his turmoil.

Holly sat down on one of the loungers. "Let me explain."

"I'd like to hear you try. How can I believe you? How can I know what's real and what isn't? Don't you see, Holly, this calls everything into question."

"At least let me try."

"Go on."

"When I first arrived in Cheston I didn't really have a plan. Talking to a girl in the Wimpy one night she suggested there was money to be earned working the area near the Masonic Lodge and snooker hall. I'd got nothing to lose so I thought I'd give it a try. It was slow at first but after a few nights things picked up. I'd go with men in their cars or sometimes they'd take a room at the hotel near the station. Ted Collins picked me up one evening early on. He was friendly, paid over the going rate and wasn't too demanding. He said that he'd see me the following week."

Holly glanced at Bruce to see if she should continue. He nodded.

"At the end of our second meeting he suddenly got aggressive, showed me his warrant card and threatened to arrest me and tell the organized ring of prostitutes who work the lorry parks where I was. That's the group pimped by Brady's sidekick. Vicious outfit."

"So that's how you knew about Pete Brady."

Holly nodded. "Collins suggested we come to an arrangement. He'd see me weekly, sort out a few generous customers from his circle for me and generally watch my back. In return, he expected me to be part of his ears and eyes network. It's why I've been able to work on my own and keep more of my earnings."

Bruce looked down at her. Holly returned his stare.

"You're disgusted by me, aren't you? It's sordid. I know that. Unforgiveable."

"It's the betrayal. That's what hurts the most."

"Bruce, I know it's awful but please hear me. I haven't betrayed you. You came onto my patch, into my world. My arrangement with Ted Collins was set up ages before you came on the scene. When he first asked me about you I answered in all innocence. I didn't know you. We hadn't even met."

Bruce was listening carefully.

"I didn't have a clue that I would be attracted to you. There I've said it. Another time, another place. Why weren't you around when my life fell apart? I haven't played you Bruce. I really haven't. My life has been about feeling trapped but these last few months it's been worse. Much worse. That night I was upset I had been with him. He'd asked me about you as I knew he would. I'd decided to tell him I couldn't talk to him about you anymore. That's when he did what he did." Holly faltered.

"It was Collins?"

Holly nodded.

"It's been difficult for me since then. He must have said something to his pals. Probably told them I'd got the clap or something. Work's tailed off with them."

Bruce sat quietly. His mind was racing. "Thanks for telling me. Holly."

"I'll go now." she said.

Bruce walked with Holly back into the house to the front door. He opened it for her and stood watching her as she walked away down the drive. She turned and gave a hesitant half wave. He raised his hand and then closed the door.

Called into Question

Chapter 33

Muir and Sophia Hammond had enjoyed their weekend in the Cotswolds with their daughters. Their cottage was in the small peaceful village of Naunton, in the rolling country between Cheltenham and Bourton-on-the-Water. There were still some true locals left in the village. Their soft Gloucestershire accent complemented the warm stone of the buildings and walls. The Hammonds spent their breaks gardening, walking and reading. They enjoyed worshipping at the little Baptist chapel that perched on the side of the valley. Muir relished not having any responsibility. He found himself able to engage with the worship more freely than when at home. The most relaxing aspect of these times away was the luxury of not being interrupted by phone calls or called out to others' domestic crises. Even the journey home winding through Northleach and Witney before picking up the motorway after Oxford had a calming effect.

Their journey home on that Sunday afternoon had been uneventful. Muir had, for once, given in to the girls' pleas to listen to the Top 40 show on Radio 1. If nothing else, it seemed to make the time pass more quickly. He pulled on to the drive and started to unload the car while Sophia and the girls went ahead in to the house. They were jockeying for first use of one of the two toilets.

"Mum! Dad! Quick! Come here. Something's happened to Bruce. He's been sick. He's not moving."

Muir Hammond could hear the panic in his youngest daughter's voice.

"Coming Hannah!" He ran upstairs. Hannah was standing at the bathroom door. Looking past her, he could see his son's legs and feet. Bruce was lying on the floor.

"Okay darling, good girl, go and get your mother, she's getting her things from the car. It's going to be alright."

"Daddy, he's not moving."

"Just do as I say. Go down and get your mother."

Bruce was sprawled on the bathroom floor. His head was resting on his arms alongside the toilet bowl. He had been sick in the toilet and on the floor.

Muir kneeled beside his son and felt for a pulse in his neck. Bruce stirred slightly. "Bruce. Can you hear me? It's dad. Come on my old son; let's get you sat up and straightened out a bit." Bruce lifted his head and turned to look at his father. He struggled to focus. Muir Hammond recoiled a little as he smelled his son's breath. Rum and vomit was never a pleasant combination.

Sophia Hammond came into the bathroom. "Oh, my boy, my Brucie. Is he alright? What's happened?"

"He's going to be fine. Can you get a strong coffee with a couple of sugars and a jug of water? I'll clean him up."

"Yes, but what's happened?"

"I think he's rather the worse for wear. Tell the girls Bruce is going to be fine. He has just been unwell. We don't need them getting hysterical. No help to anyone."

Muir helped Bruce to sit up with his back resting against the bath. He wiped his face with a flannel and gave him a glass of water.

"I haven't done this for anyone since my student days." he said. "Or had it done for me for that matter."

Bruce became slightly more with it. "Sorry for mess. Stupid mess."

"Don't worry. Nothing that can't be cleaned up. Let's get you into bed."

"Can't be cleaned up. Big mess." Bruce shook his head slowly, almost comically.

His parents helped Bruce into his room and put him to bed. His record player was turning, the LP he had played crackling at the end of the last track. An empty dark rum bottle was on the floor. A brown bottle of aspirin lay on its side on the bedside cabinet. The cotton wool and half a dozen tablets had spilled out. The bottle was still half full.

Sophia Hammond looked at the mess. "Muir, you don't think Bruce, you know tried to...." Her voice tailed off

"I doubt it. We can talk in the morning. He needs to sleep this off. Why don't you go down and be with the girls?"

Bruce's mother bent down and kissed him on the forehead. "My poor Brucie. You are such a worry."

"Down you go, darling. Leave him be. He'll be fine." said Muir reassuringly.

When he was sure his wife was downstairs Bruce's father shook him firmly to rouse him from the sleep in to which he was slipping. "Bruce, Bruce. Listen this is important. You can sleep in a while. You must tell me. Have you taken tablets?"

Bruce nodded.

"How many Bruce? Try and think carefully?"

"Only two or three." he mumbled.

"Are you sure? I need to know if you've taken more."

"No, only two or three Dad. Had a headache."

"Okay. Go to sleep now. I'm leaving the door open and the landing light on.

Your mum and I will be listening out."

Bruce smiled slightly. "Like when I was little." he muttered.

"Yes, like when you were little." His father sighed. "We'll talk in the morning."

His father took a mop and a bucket of Dettol and water to the bathroom before joining his wife downstairs. "I think he'll have quite a hangover in the morning. I'd like him to go and see Dr. Adams at the surgery."

After Bruce had watched Holly walk away earlier that afternoon he had gone back into the garden and sat on the ground leaning against an old apple tree. His thoughts were scrambled. He went back over the last few months, trying to remember details, replaying every conversation he had shared with Holly. The exchanges with DCI Collins were easier to pin down and recall. As he combed through all his recollections he could feel his anger shift away from Holly and on to Collins. What a devious bastard that man was!

After a while he had taken the tea things into the house. He scraped the sandwiches and untouched cake straight into the dustbin by the back door. He put three copies of the Cheston Observer into the bin to cover the discarded food. He had gone up to his room. The ringing in his ears, the hollow sensation had become a full-blown headache. He had taken the bottle of aspirin from the medicine cabinet in the bathroom and swallowed three without reading the label.

Going back in to his room he took a swig of rum to help the tablets on their way. He put Bowie's *Aladdin Sane* on with the volume down. Then he had started drinking and continued until he finished the bottle. The last thing he remembered was getting up to be ill.

The following morning Bruce did not attempt to come down to breakfast until his sisters had all set off for school. His father joined him at the breakfast table a coffee mug in hand.

"I should think you're feeling rough, aren't you?"

"Yes, dad. Just a bit. I am sorry for making a mess."

"It's ok. Not the first time I've done that duty and who knows, may not be the last. Took me back to my student days."

"I thought you'd always been teetotal."

"Ah well, there's lots about their parents that children don't know and vice versa. It's how we all survive. Let me say simply that as because of my first two years of art school in London teetotalism became a logical step! Now let's talk about you, shall we?"

"If we must."

"I think we should. I've phoned the surgery and Dr. Adams is happy to see

Called into Question 251

you at the end of the morning. I know you'll probably be unhappy that I've done this without talking to you, but your mother and I are concerned for you. You've had to deal with a lot in these last few weeks. The accident alone was upsetting but being shot on top of that would test the strongest of men. There is no shame in admitting that you're feeling the pressure."

Bruce sat at the table. He said nothing.

"I'll run you up there once you've showered and dressed."

"Thanks Dad."

Dr. Adams had known the family since their arrival from London. He had seen Bruce mature from the gangly youth of a few years ago to the young police officer sitting before him that morning. He gave Bruce a basic examination and then asked him some questions. He gave him a chance to talk about how he felt about the accident and the shooting. To Bruce's embarrassment he asked him about the pattern of his drinking and sexual behaviour. Bruce confirmed that one was out of control and the other nonexistent.

Dr. Adams brought the consultation to a close. "As far as I can see you're healing well physically from the shooting. Mr. Gannon was right when he said you'd make a full recovery. I am much less happy about your psychological health. Since we've had our troops over in Northern Ireland the army has been taking combat stress much more seriously. They have identified that men who have been shot by snipers often suffer from delayed shock. I am certain that is what has happened to you. I could prescribe you a short course of Valium, but I would rather hold that back in reserve. It works but some of my colleagues are dubious about the long-term effects. Bruce, I think you'd benefit from some straight-forward counselling. Your recent traumas have had an effect and that makes it hard for you to deal with any other emotional pressures in your life. Would you be prepared to give counselling a try?"

Bruce looked thoughtful as he sat there. He suspected that his father had briefed their GP rather fully. He was not keen on the prospect of medication.

"I'll give it a try Doctor."

"Good I'm glad to hear it. I think if you approach it with an open mind and see it as a chance to offload you will benefit from it. I am going to sign you off work for another month. That should give you the space you need. Your father is right. There is no shame in this, whatsoever. On the contrary, I hear you've been very courageous."

Bruce shrugged, stood up, shook the doctor's offered hand and left the room.

Initially Bruce was surprised to have been signed off for an additional period but the more he thought about it he realized that he felt a huge sense of relief. He allowed himself plenty of rest, began to read and enjoyed listening to three new albums. He was also able to increase the amount of exercise he undertook.

His first visit to the psychologist was fixed for just two weeks after his appointment with the GP. He really did not know what to expect from the sessions. He was pleasantly surprised to find they were relaxed meetings. The questions he was asked were non-threatening and made it easy for him to talk. The psychologist made it clear from the outset that their discussions would be completely confidential. There would be no report to anyone in the force. Bruce found this hugely liberating. He realized how much he had bottled up over the previous year.

* * * *

About three weeks into his extended absence Harpal Shaik rang Bruce at home one evening.

"Hello my friend. How's it going? I've been missing our chats and my squash is distinctly rusty. Lots of the guys on the shift were asking after you. They asked me to pass on their best wishes if I was in touch."

"That's kind. How are things at the nick?"

"Settling down after that mad few days. Normal stuff but I haven't rung up to talk about work. The shift is on relief cover next week which means of course I've got two days off. I wondered if you fancy going over to Windsor, we could take a boat out."

"Thanks mate. That would be great. I am beginning to get a touch of camp fever being in the barracks too much." Bruce appreciated his friend's thoughtfulness.

"Great. I'll pick you up about two o'clock on Tuesday."

*   *   *   *

Harpal parked in a car park near the railway arches. They walked through the public gardens to the landing stage just below the bridge to Eton.

"When we first moved here you could still get a bus over the bridge." said Bruce.

"I remember. I think it's better since they shut it off. At least the Japanese tourists are less of a hazard! Let's take one of the motor boats. I'll sort the deposit."

"Are you sure?"

"Yes fine," said Harpal, a little distracted by the pedestrians on the steps leading down from the bridge.

The young lad working the boats, no doubt as his father had done before him, steadied the motor-boat as Bruce clambered in to the back. Harpal followed and sat in the front behind the wheel. Just as the lad was about to push them out into the river Harpal said, "Well look who's here?"

Bruce barely had time to register what was going on before Holly skipped nimbly from the path onto the landing stage and into the boat. She steadied herself with one arm on Harpal's shoulder before sitting herself down next to Bruce. The little red boat rocked unsteadily.

"What the blazes are you doing here? Oh, I get it. Harpal do you know anything about this?"

Harpal turned flashed a smile and winked.

"Hello Bruce. Hi Harpal. Well this is nice isn't it!" chortled Holly.

"Great I've been stitched up again. Story of my life."

"Don't be cross with Harpal, Bruce." said Holly leaning against him playfully.

Harpal was concentrating on avoiding one of the pleasure launches. He headed upstream towards Boveney lock. As the river traffic thinned out he said, "Bruce sorry to trick you. I thought it was about time we got together, three outsiders if ever there were."

"How did you get in touch with Miss Brewer here?"
"We met at the hospital. Holly recognized me and gave me her number, so she could keep in touch with how you are doing." Holly blushed slightly.

"Well I don't know what to say?"

"Another of those rare moments in history when Bruce Hammond does not know what to say." laughed Harpal. "Well how about we just enjoy the scenery for a while. Let's imagine we've won the football pools and choose one of these houses to buy."

They headed upstream, surveying the glamorous properties with boat houses and manicured lawns running to the water's edge. Bruce leaned his head back, closed his eyes and trailed his hand in the cool water. Holly leaned more closely against Bruce and whispered. "Don't be cross Bruce. Please forgive me."

Bruce looked at her, said nothing but to Holly's encouragement he smiled and held her gaze. They motored along gently in companionable silence. When they reached the weir Harpal turned the boat round. "Either of you two fancy taking the controls?"

"No, we're fine thanks, if you're ok." said Holly smiling. Harpal noticed she had linked her arm through Bruce's.

"Well I'm glad we're a happy crew," said Harpal, "that's how it should be. Life's too short to be out of sorts with friends."

Bruce laughed. "You do come out with some quaint phrases sometimes O wise one!"

"Blame it on my colonial heritage Sahib," retorted Harpal, "which of course means it is *your* fault! Anyway, I have an announcement to make, two in fact. You are now both aware that I am engaged to a young lady called Padmakshi. I am delighted to tell you that a date has been fixed for our marriage next spring."

"Wow that is news, Harpal. Do I congratulate you or commiserate?" said Bruce half-jokingly. Holly elbowed him in the ribs.

"Ow. Watch it. I've been shot you know!"

"Sorry Bruce. I forgot." said Holly looking anxious.

"It's alright just joking." Holly elbowed him again. "Seriously Harpal, when was this fixed?"

"Officially last week, but I have been thinking about it for a couple of months. Padmakshi is lovely. The more time I have spent with her the more confident I've become that we could be good for each other."

"Well good for you. What was the second announcement?"

"It's also about Padmakshi and me. In our discussions, we have decided that she is not going to join my family's business. Instead she is going to set up her own accountancy practice." Harpal looked over his shoulder and smiled proudly.

"Congratulations!" said Holly.

"Yes, well done, mate. Smart move. You please the family on the one hand and then surprise them on the other." Bruce was impressed with his friend's decisions.
"What about you two?" asked Harpal.

Bruce and Holly looked at each other. After a few moments of silence, they both started to speak at the same time. "Ladies first," said Bruce indicating that Holly should continue.

"Harpal I know what you mean, and you're very kind. This is great being able to be together. I'm sure that Bruce agrees the last time we saw each other was not our finest moment. "

"That's an understatement." said Bruce smiling as he splashed Holly playfully with a handful of water.

Holly continued. "I have been doing lots of thinking too. I've made a decision which I hope you'll both approve of. I'm going to leave Cheston. I have applied to do a diploma in Art & Design at an art college."

Harpal cheered, "Holly that's great well done. Brilliant news."

"Yes, that is great," said Bruce hurriedly. "Which college are you going to?"

"It's in Falmouth." replied Holly enthusiastically.

"Falmouth in Cornwall? That's a long way." Bruce looked thoughtful.

"What other Falmouth is there? I figured that if I was going to make a fresh start I should go somewhere completely new. I still get the small allowance from my dad's estate and I hope to get a grant."

"Well good for you, Holly. Good for you. I'm really pleased." Bruce hugged her, looking downstream over her shoulder as he did so.

"So that just leaves you Bruce, the last one standing. What are you going to do? Have you made up your mind with all this time to think?" Harpal glanced over his shoulder again to look at his friend.

"Sorry not to be able to complete the set. I am still unsure to be honest. My sessions with the shrink are going well. She suggested I should take my time. I've got a few ideas. I think it's unlikely that I'll stay in the police, but I don't want to resign until I know what I am going on to."

"That sounds wise," said Holly squeezing his arm.

"I have a meeting with the Divisional Superintendent next week. That will be interesting to say the least. In any case whatever I choose to do I can't go far from here until the trials are over. That could be months yet."

By this time, they had arrived back in Windsor. Harpal cut the engine and they drifted alongside the landing stage. The young lad reached out with his boathook, pulled them in and helped them ashore.

Chapter 34

August 28th

Harpal's plan worked. He's a good guy. Bruce wasn't angry. It was a lovely afternoon on the river. Harpal has set a date for the wedding. I told them my plan. They seemed happy for me. Bruce hugged me and said he was really pleased. I will miss him. Another time, another place might have been different. He hasn't decided what to do. New beginnings.

Auntie Sally wrote back – they are pleased. They want me to go there in the holidays – not sure about that. She wants to tell my mum – I've said no. Worrying news is Ann-Marie has gone missing. Not been seen for a week. One of the other girls found her knife – had blood on it. Hope she is ok. Glad I am getting out.

Chapter 35

Bruce had only met the Divisional commander, Superintendent Baxter, briefly on one previous occasion shortly after arriving in Cheston. That had been little more than a courtesy call.

After weeks of having been at home it felt strange to be back in uniform, if only for a morning. He was glad to have been cleared by the doctor to drive again. Driving into Cheston across the bridge over the Thames Bruce was conscious of just how much had happened since he had first driven to Eynsham Hall on that autumn morning a year ago.

In his last session with the psychologist he had reflected on the ways in which he had changed since joining the police. Together they had concluded that the experiences had impacted on Bruce considerably. On balance, he felt that the gains outweighed the losses. He was more worldly-wise and viewed the world less through rose-tinted spectacles. His confidence had taken a major knock for a while but in recent weeks he had begun to feel more positive. Some of the tests and activities that he undertook in the sessions indicated that he still held strong principles, but these were now tempered with less demanding expectations of those around him. Bruce hoped he had become a better listener through having good listening modeled to him by Inspector Middleton, Holly and his psychologist. He had also appreciated the work he had done on anger management in some of the later sessions. He liked to think he was more self-aware and more controlled now. Time would tell.

It was Inspector Middleton who had rung to tell Bruce about the meeting with the Superintendent. Bruce had no doubt that Bob Middleton would have provided a full briefing for the superior officer. He expected to be pressed as to his plans. Ever since the conversation on the river with Holly and Harpal he had felt a degree of envy that his two friends now had clear ideas about their future whereas he was still casting around for direction. He was still struggling to make sense of Holly's warmth towards him contrasting with her decision to make a new start, hundreds of miles away.

The Superintendent had a large airy office on the second floor in the administration block. A large window looked south and gave a fine view of Windsor Castle. Bruce could see even from this distance that the Royal Standard was flying; Her Majesty was in residence. He wondered if she ever looked across the meadows and the playing fields of Eton at Bruce and his colleagues going about their business, like ants maintaining law and order in her name.

Bruce went into the office when summoned and sat down in one of two comfortable chairs by a coffee table. The superintendent came around from behind his desk and sat in the other chair. He opened the conversation by asking after Bruce's health.

"I am doing well thank you sir. I hope I might be able to start playing squash again in a month or two. I have missed the exercise and the competition." said Bruce. "I have also been having some counselling, actually therapy would be a more accurate description to help me deal with the shock of the shooting and the accident." He had decided in advance that he would talk about this aspect of his recovery if it seemed appropriate. He looked carefully at the Superintendent to see how he would react to this disclosure.

"I am glad to hear it," said Superintendent Baxter. He sounded genuine in his reaction. "I wish more officers would take up that opportunity. I suspect that over the coming years it will become more commonplace. We really do have to deal with society's rubbish don't we, PC Hammond." Baxter seemed more enlightened than Bruce had expected him to be.

"I understand from Inspector Middleton that you may be planning to resign from the force. Is that the case?"

"Yes, sir. I have been wondering if I am cut out for it."

"Well let me assure you on that front Bruce. I think you are eminently suited to modern policing. I have no doubt that you must have serious misgivings about whether that's so, not least as you have encountered very different attitudes among some of your colleagues and superiors."

Bruce nodded but said nothing.

"Bob Middleton tells me that you are a resourceful, intelligent and thoughtful young man. He is someone whose opinion I value highly, so well done for impressing him. I gather you have thought about some of the deeper issues that underpin our approach to policing. Our work is going to become more technical. We will have to work harder to keep people's respect and trust. Without those things, we will effectively lose our mandate from ordinary people to maintain law and order. If that happens there is a real danger that the Police Force nationally will become more politicized. Are you following PC Hammond?"

"Very much so, sir. To be honest it encourages me to hear you say this."

"I thought it might. You don't really need me to tell you that there are quite a few senior officers in our force, some of whom you have had the misfortune to meet, who cannot begin to grasp these issues. PC Hammond, I am about to tell you two things which I hope will encourage you even more and which may help you come to a decision about your future. The first is something which once I have said it I will not be able to discuss further. You must treat it as highly confidential. Indeed, I might even forget I have said it to you. The second is something which I hope you will want to discuss."

The Superintendent looked closely at Bruce. "I hope you have understood. Please listen very closely." Bruce was fascinated; he had not expected the conversation to unfold like this. He had not been prepared to be taken into his commanding officer's confidence.

"I am led to believe that a certain well-known officer, one might even say a notorious gentleman is currently subject to a high-level investigation about possible corrupt practices and links to criminals living abroad. It appears that this individual put some noses out of joint among our London friends. They have not got mad, but it seems they are about to get even. The gentleman in question was officially suspended on full pay as of 22.00 hours last night. I shall say no more." Superintendent Baxter paused to allow Bruce to assimilate this information.

Bruce took a moment or two thinking about what he had been told. Then he smiled. "Thank you, sir, for telling me that. I shall be happy to keep it to myself."

The older man smiled back. "Good. Well I hope that neither of us have to wait too long before we can discuss it with colleagues who will welcome the news as we both do. The second thing has even more bearing on your personal circumstances. I have already talked about the demands and direction of policing over the next twenty years or so. There are going to be some interesting developments in the training courses being offered at the national police college at Bramshill. Some of the universities are also beginning to do some innovative work in this field. For example, did you know Bruce that Keele University has launched a degree course in Criminology as part of its sociology department?"

Bruce shook his head. "No sir."

"There is interest in this at the highest level, and I mean the highest level nationally. It seems to me and one or two influential officers above me that someone such as yourself would be an ideal candidate to take up a sponsored place on that course. The details have yet to be worked out, but it would probably operate rather like a secondment. If you take up this offer you would be like a normal student in term time. You would be paid at a basic rate and be expected to undertake certain duties during the holidays. How does that sound?"

"I don't know what to say sir."

"You don't have to say anything at this stage. I hope you will think about it seriously and let Inspector Middleton know your answer before you return to duties. I have given him some of the paperwork. He will be able to answer any other questions. Thank you for your time PC Hammond. I hope to see you again. Good luck with whatever you choose to do."

"Thank you, sir."

Bruce drove home, his head spinning with new possibilities. On the edge of town, he pulled up by the phone box where he had arrested the young hoaxer. He went in dialed the number and waited for the connection. He heard the pips and put his coin in. "It's me. Guess what?"

The End

Printed in Great Britain
by Amazon